MURDER MOST UNLADYLIKE

MURDER MOST UNLADYLIKE

A WELLS & WONG MYSTERY

ROBIN STEVENS

CORGI BOOKS

MURDER MOST UNLADYLIKE: A WELLS & WONG MYSTERY
A CORGI BOOK 978 0 552 57072 5

First published in Great Britain by Corgi Books,
an imprint of Random House Children's Publishers UK
A Random House Group Company

This edition published 2014

9 10

The Random House Group Limited supports the Forest Stewardship Council®
(FSC®), the leading international forest-certification organisation. Our books
carrying the FSC label are printed on FSC®-certified paper. FSC is the only
forest-certification scheme supported by the leading environmental organisations,
including Greenpeace. Our paper procurement policy can be found at
www.randomhouse.co.uk/environment

Set in ITC New Baskerville

Corgi Books are published by Random House Children's Publishers UK
61–63 Uxbridge Road, London W5 5SA

www.randomhousechildrens.co.uk
www.totallyrandombooks.co.uk
www.randomhouse.co.uk

Addresses for companies within The Random House Group Limited
can be found at: www.randomhouse.co.uk/offices.htm

THE RANDOM HOUSE GROUP Limited Reg. No. 954009

A CIP catalogue record for this book is available from the British Library.

Printed and bound by CPI Group (UK) Ltd, Croydon, CR0 4YY

To all the school friends
who became my other family,
and to Miss Silk and Mrs Sanderson,
who would never have murdered anyone.

MURDER MOST UNLADYLIKE

Being an account of

The Case of the Murder of Miss Bell,
an investigation by the Wells and Wong Detective Society.

Written by Hazel Wong
(Detective Society Secretary), aged 13.

Begun Tuesday 30th October 1934.

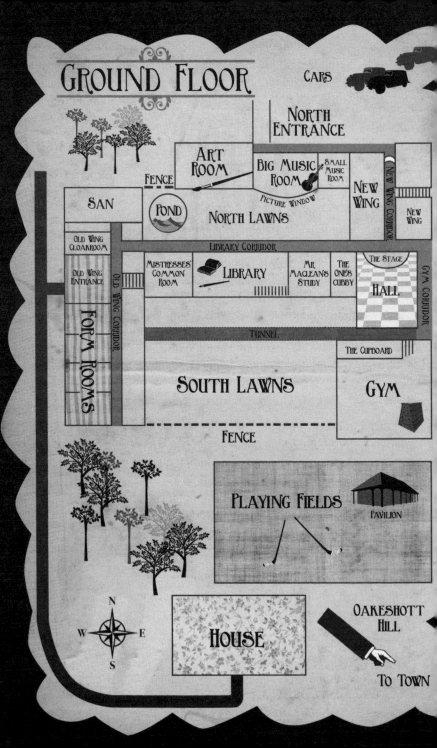

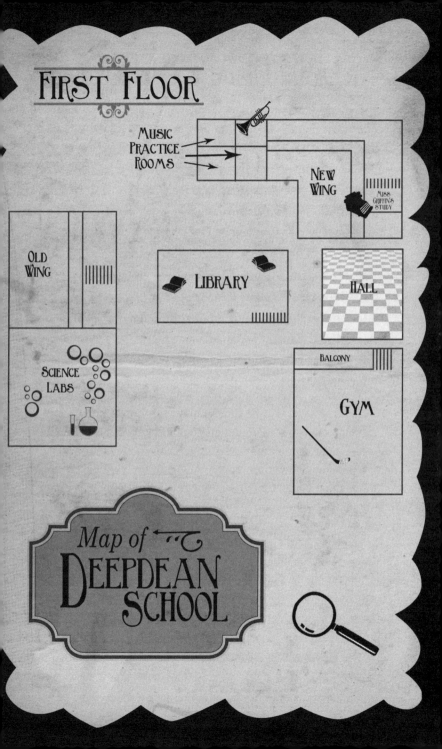

DEEPDEAN SCHOOL

THE STAFF

Miss Griffin – *Headmistress*

Miss Lappet – *History and Latin mistress*

Miss Bell – *Science mistress, also the victim*

Miss Parker – *Maths mistress*

Mr MacLean – *Reverend*

Mr Reid, 'The One' – *Music and Art master*

Miss Tennyson – *English mistress*

Miss Hopkins – *Games mistress*

Mademoiselle Renauld, 'Mamzelle' – *French mistress*

Mrs Minn, 'Minny' – *Nurse*

Mr Jones – *Handyman*

Matron – *Matron*

THE GIRLS

Daisy Wells – *Third former and President of the Wells & Wong Detective Society*
Hazel Wong – *Third former and Secretary of the Wells & Wong Detective Society*

THIRD FORMERS

Kitty Freebody
Rebecca 'Beanie' Martineau
Lavinia Temple
Clementine Delacroix
Sophie Croke-Finchley

FIRST FORMER

Betsy North

SECOND FORMERS

Binny Freebody
The Marys

FIFTH FORMER

Alice Murgatroyd

BIG GIRLS

Virginia Overton
Belinda Vance

HEAD GIRL

Henrietta Trilling, 'King Henry'

PART ONE

THE DISCOVERY
OF THE BODY

1

This is the first murder that the Wells & Wong Detective Society has ever investigated, so it is a good thing Daisy bought me a new casebook. The last one was finished after we solved The Case of Lavinia's Missing Tie. The solution to that, of course, was that Clementine stole it in revenge for Lavinia punching her in the stomach during lacrosse, which was Lavinia's revenge for Clementine telling everyone Lavinia came from a broken home. I suspect that the solution to this new case may be more complex.

I suppose I ought to give some explanation of ourselves, in honour of the new casebook. Daisy Wells is the President of the Detective Society, and I, Hazel Wong, am its Secretary. Daisy says that this makes her Sherlock Holmes, and me Watson. This is probably fair. After all, I am much too short to be the heroine of this story, and who ever heard of a Chinese Sherlock Holmes?

That's why it's so funny that it was me who found Miss Bell's dead body. In fact, I think Daisy is still upset about it, though of course she pretends not to be. You see, Daisy is a heroine-like person, and so it should be her that these things happen to.

Look at Daisy and you think you know exactly the sort of person she is – one of those dainty, absolutely English girls with blue eyes and golden hair; the kind who'll gallop across muddy fields in the rain clutching hockey sticks and then sit down and eat ten iced buns at tea. I, on the other hand, bulge all over like Bibendum the Michelin Man; my cheeks are moony-round and my hair and eyes are stubbornly dark brown.

I arrived from Hong Kong part way through second form, and even then, when we were all still shrimps (*shrimps*, for this new casebook, is what we call the little lower-form girls), Daisy was already famous throughout Deepdean School. She rode horses, was part of the lacrosse team, and was a member of the Drama Society. The Big Girls took notice of her, and by May the entire school knew that the Head Girl herself had called Daisy a 'good sport'.

But that is only the outside of Daisy, the jolly-good-show part that everyone sees. The inside of her is not jolly-good-show at all.

It took me quite a while to discover that.

2

Daisy wants me to explain what happened this term up to the time I found the body. She says that is what proper detectives do – add up the evidence first – so I will. She also says that a good Secretary should keep her casebook on her at all times to be ready to write up important events as they happen. It was no good reminding her that I do that anyway.

The most important thing to happen in those first few weeks of the autumn term was the Detective Society, and it was Daisy who began that. Daisy is all for making up societies for things. Last year we had the Pacifism Society (dull) and then the Spiritualism Society (less dull, but then Lavinia smashed her mug during a séance, Beanie fainted and Matron banned spiritualism altogether).

But that was all last year, when we were still shrimps.

We can't be messing about with silly things like ghosts now that we are grown-up third formers – that was what Daisy said when she came back at the beginning of this term having discovered crime.

I was quite glad. Not that I was ever afraid of ghosts, exactly. Everyone knows there aren't any. Even so, there are enough ghost stories going round our school to horrify anybody. The most famous of our ghosts is Verity Abraham, the girl who committed suicide off the Gym balcony the term before I arrived at Deepdean, but there are also ghosts of an ex-mistress who locked herself into one of the music rooms and starved herself to death, and a little first-form shrimp who drowned in the pond.

As I said, Daisy decided that this year we were going to be detectives. She arrived at House with her tuck box full of books with sinister, shadowy covers and titles like *Peril at End House* and *Mystery Mile*. Matron confiscated them one by one, but Daisy always managed to find more.

We started the Detective Society in the first week of term. The two of us made a deadly secret pact that no one else, not even our dorm mates, Kitty, Beanie and Lavinia, could be told about it. It did make me feel proud, just me and Daisy having a secret. It was awfully fun too, creeping about behind the others' backs and pretending to be ordinary when all the time *we* knew we were detectives on a secret mission to obtain information.

Daisy set all our first detective missions. In that first week we crept into the other third-form dorm and read Clementine's secret journal, and then Daisy chose a first former and set us to find out everything we could about her. This, Daisy told me, was practice – just like memorizing the licences of every motor car we saw.

In our second week there was the case of why King Henry (our name for this year's Head Girl, Henrietta Trilling, because she is so remote and regal, and has such beautiful chestnut curls) wasn't at Prayers one morning. But it only took a few hours before everyone, not just us, knew that she had been sent a telegram saying that her aunt had died suddenly that morning.

'Poor thing,' said Kitty, when we found out. Kitty has the next-door bed to Daisy's in our dorm, and Daisy has designated her a Friend of the Detective Society, even though she is still not allowed to know about it. She has smooth, light brown hair and masses of freckles, and she keeps something hidden in the bottom of her tuck box that I thought at first was a torture device but turned out to be eyelash curlers. She is as mad about gossip as Daisy, though for less scientific reasons. 'Poor old King Henry. She hasn't had much luck. She was Verity Abraham's best friend, after all, and *you* know what happened to Verity. She hasn't been the same since.'

'I don't,' said Beanie, who sleeps next to me. Her real name is Rebecca but we call her Beanie because she is very small, and everything frightens her. Lessons frighten her most of all, though. She says that when she looks at a page all the letters and numbers get up and do a jig until she can't think straight. 'What did happen to Verity?'

'*She killed herself*,' said Kitty in annoyance. 'Jumped off the Gym balcony last year. Come on, Beans.'

'Oh!' said Beanie. 'Of course. I always thought she tripped.'

Sometimes Beanie is quite slow.

Something else happened at the beginning of term that turned out to be very important indeed: The One arrived.

You see, at the end of last year Miss Nelson, the Deputy Headmistress and our dull old Music and Art mistress, retired. We were expecting her to be replaced by someone else quite as uninteresting – but the new Music and Art master, Mr Reid, was not uninteresting at all. He was also not old.

Mr Reid had rugged cheekbones and a dashing moustache, and he slicked his hair back with brillantine. He looked exactly like a film star, although nobody could agree on which one. Kitty thought Douglas Fairbanks Jr, and Clementine said Clark Gable, but only because Clementine is obsessed with Clark Gable. Really though, it did not matter. Mr Reid was a man, and he was not Mr MacLean (our dotty, unwashed old Reverend whom Kitty calls Mr MacDirty), and so the whole school fell in love with him at once.

A deadly serious half-secret Society dedicated to the worship of Mr Reid was established by Kitty. At its first meeting, he was rechristened The One. We all had to go about making the secret signal at each other (index finger raised, right eye winking) whenever we were in His Presence.

The One had barely been at Deepdean for a week when he caused the biggest shock since Verity last year.

You see, before this term, the whole school knew that Miss Bell (our Science mistress) and Miss Parker (our Maths mistress) had a secret. They lived together in Miss Parker's little flat in town, which had a spare room in it. The spare room was the secret. I did not understand when Daisy first told me about the spare room; now we are in the third form, though, of course I see exactly what it must mean. It has something to do with Miss Parker's hair, cut far too short even to be fashionable, and the way she and Miss Bell used to pass their cigarettes from one to the other during bunbreaks last year.

There were no cigarettes being passed this term, though, because on the first day Miss Bell took one look at The One and fell for him as madly as Kitty did.

This was a terrible shock. Miss Bell was not considered a beauty. She was very tucked-in and buttoned-up and severe in her white lab coat. And she was poor. Miss Bell wore the same three threadbare blouses on rotation, cut her own hair and did secretarial work for Miss Griffin after school hours for extra pay. Everyone rather pitied her, and we assumed The One would too. We were astonished when he did not.

'Something has clearly *happened* between them,' Clementine told our form at the end of the first week of term. 'I went to the science lab during bunbreak and I came upon Miss Bell and The One *canoodling*. It was really shocking!'

'I bet they weren't, really,' said Lavinia scornfully. Lavinia is part of our dorm, too – she is a big, heavy girl with a stubborn mop of dark hair, and most of the time she is unhappy.

'They were!' said Clementine. 'I know what it looks like. I saw my brother doing the same thing last month.'

I couldn't stop myself blushing. Imagining stiff, well-starched Miss Bell *canoodling* (whatever that meant) was extraordinarily awkward.

Then Miss Parker got to hear about it. Miss Parker is truly ferocious, with chopped-short black hair and a furious voice that comes bellowing out of her tiny body like a foghorn. The row was immense. Almost the whole school heard it, and the upshot was that Miss Bell was not allowed to live in the little flat any more.

Then, at the beginning of the second week of term, everything changed again. We could barely keep up with it all. Suddenly The One no longer seemed to want to spend time with Miss Bell. Instead, he began to take up with Miss Hopkins.

Miss Hopkins is our Games mistress. She is round and relentlessly cheerful (unless you happen not to be good at Games) and she marches about the school corridors brandishing a hockey stick, her athletic brown hair always coming down from its fashionable clipped-back waves. She *is* pretty, and (I think) quite young, so it was not at all surprising that The One should notice her – it was only shocking that he should jilt Miss Bell to do it.

So now it was The One and Miss Hopkins seen canoodling in form rooms, and all Miss Bell could do was storm past them whenever she saw them, her lips pursed and her glare freezing.

General Deepdean opinion was against Miss Bell. Miss Hopkins was pretty while Miss Bell was not, and Miss Hopkins's father was a very important magistrate in Gloucestershire while Miss Bell's was nothing important at all. But I could not help being on Miss Bell's side. After all, it was not *her* fault that The One had jilted her, and she could not help being poor.

Now that she could not stay in the flat, of course, she was poorer than ever, and that made me worry.

The only thing Miss Bell had to cheer her up was the Deputy Headmistress job, and even that was not the consolation it should have been. You see, Miss Griffin had to appoint a new Deputy, and after a few weeks the rumour went round that Miss Bell was about to be chosen. This ought to have been lucky – once she was formally appointed, Miss Bell's money worries would vanish for good – but all it really meant was that the mistresses who were not chosen began to despise her. There were two others really in the running. The first was Miss Tennyson, our English mistress – that is her name, really, although she is no relation to the famous one. If you've seen that painting of the Lady of Shalott drooping in her boat, you have seen Miss Tennyson. Her hair is always down round her face, and she is as drippy as underdone cake. The second was Miss Lappet, our History and Latin mistress, who is grey and useless and shaped like an overstuffed cushion, but *thinks* she is Miss Griffin's most trusted adviser. They were both simply fuming about the Deputy Headmistress job, and snubbed Miss Bell in the corridor whenever they saw her.

And then the murder happened.

3

I say that it was me who found the body of Miss Bell, and it was, but I never would have been there at all if it hadn't been for those crime novels of Daisy's. Matron's fondness for confiscation meant that it was no good trying to read them up at House, so Daisy took to hanging around down at school in the evenings. She joined the Literature Society, slipped *Whose Body?* between the pages of *Paradise Lost*, and sat there peacefully reading it while the others talked. I joined too, and sat at the back of the room writing up my Detective Society case notes. Everyone thought I was writing poetry.

It was after Lit. Soc, on Monday 29th October, that it happened. After-school societies end at 5.20, but afterwards Daisy and I hung back in the empty form room so that she could finish *The Man in the Queue*. Daisy was absorbed, but I was jumpy with worry that we might be late for dinner up at House and thus incur the awful wrath of Matron. I looked about for my pullover and then remembered with annoyance where I had left it.

'Bother,' I said. 'Daisy, my pullover's in the Gym. Wait for me, I'll just be a minute.'

Daisy, nose in her book as usual, shrugged vaguely to show that she had heard and continued reading. I looked at my wristwatch again and saw that it was 5.40. If I ran, I'd have just enough time, as getting up to House from Old Wing Entrance takes seven minutes, and dinner is at six o'clock exactly.

I pelted along the empty, chalk-smelling corridor of Old Wing, and then turned right down the high, black and white tiled Library corridor, my feet echoing in the hush and my chest heaving. Even after a year at Deepdean, when I run, I still huff and puff in a way that rude Miss Hopkins calls 'determinedly unladylike'.

I passed the mistresses' common room, the library, Mr MacLean's study, The One's cubby and the Hall, and then turned right again onto the corridor that leads to the Gym. There's a school legend that the Gym is haunted by the ghost of Verity Abraham. When I first heard it I was younger, and I believed it. I imagined Verity all bloody, with her long hair hanging down in front of her face, wearing her pinafore and tie and holding a lacrosse stick.

Even now that I am older and not a shrimp any more,

just knowing that I am on my way to the Gym gives me the shivers. It does not help that the Gym corridor is awful. It's packed full of dusty, broken bits of old school furniture that stand up like people in the gloom. That evening all the lights were off, and everything was smudged in murky shades of grey and brown. I ran very fast down the corridor, pushed open the doors to the Gym and galumphed in, wheezing.

And there on the floor was Miss Bell.

Our Gym, in case you have not seen it for yourself, is very large, with bars and beams all folded up against the walls and wide glass windows. There's a terrifyingly high-up viewing balcony on the side nearest the main door (we are not allowed to go up there alone in case we fall, but since Verity jumped off it no one wants to), and a little room under that for us to change and leave kit in, which we call the Cupboard.

Miss Bell was lying beneath the balcony, quite still, with her arm thrown back behind her head, and her legs folded under her. In my first moment of shock it did not occur to me that she was dead. I thought I was about to get an awful ticking-off for being somewhere I oughtn't, and nearly ran away again before she caught sight of me. But then I wondered – what was Miss Bell doing, lying there like that?

I ran forward and knelt down beside her. I hesitated before touching her, because I had never touched a mistress before, but in the event it only felt like touching a human being.

I patted the shoulder of her white lab coat, hoping most awfully that she would open her eyes and sit up and scold me for being in the Gym after hours. But instead, my patting made Miss Bell's head loll away from me. Her glasses slid down off her nose and I saw that what I had thought was only a shadow behind her head was actually a dark stain the size of my handkerchief. Some of the stain had spread to the collar of her lab coat, and that part of it was red. I put out my finger and touched the stain, and my finger came away covered in blood.

I scrambled backwards, scrubbing my hand against my skirt in horror. It left a long dark smear, and I looked at that and then at Miss Bell, who had still not moved, and felt sick as anything. I had never seen a dead body up close before, but I was quite certain now that Miss Bell was dead.

What I ought to do in the circumstances was scream, I thought, but everything was so dark and quiet around me that I couldn't. What I truly wanted to do was tear off my skirt, just to get that blood away from me, but my Deepdean training rose up inside me, making the thought of running about the school half naked somehow far worse than being alone with a corpse.

As I thought this, I realized that Miss Bell really *was* dead, and I was alone with her body. I suddenly remembered the ghost of Verity Abraham, and thought that perhaps it was *her* who had killed Miss Bell, pushing her off from exactly the same spot she had jumped from a year ago . . . and now she might be waiting to do the same to me. It was silly and childish, but all the hairs prickled up on the back of my neck and, Deepdean training or no, I jumped to my feet and ran out of the Gym as fast as I could – as if Miss Bell was going to leap up and run after me.

4

I was in such a tearing hurry that as I ran back along the corridor I crashed into several abandoned chairs and scraped my knee quite badly. But I hardly noticed until later. My footsteps were echoing all around me, and dark odd-shaped shadows rose up at the edges of my vision; my breath caught in my throat. I ran all the way back along Library corridor to Old Wing and found Daisy, at last, coming out of the form room where I'd left her.

I must have looked a horrible sight, all pink and damp and heaving.

Daisy blinked at me curiously. 'Whatever's up with you? You're bleeding. We're going to be late for dinner. VO's raging about it.'

I looked down at myself in surprise, and only then saw that I had blood running down my leg from a long cut on my knee. I could not feel it at all. It was as though it had happened to another person entirely.

'Daisy,' I gasped, 'Miss Bell's dead.'

Daisy laughed. 'Oh, very funny, Hazel,' she said. 'Imagine!'

'Daisy,' I said, 'this is real. She's dead. She's in the Gym, just lying there—'

Daisy stared at me for a moment, one eyebrow raised, and that was exactly when Virginia Overton came storming out of the classroom behind her and discovered us standing there.

Virginia Overton is who Daisy meant by *VO*. She is the Monday night prefect on duty, the Big Girl who makes sure we all get back up to House after socs, and she takes her duties very seriously. She pounds about on her fat flat feet like a policeman, and presses her clipboard to her chest like an officer's notebook.

'Wells!' she snapped, looming out of the form-room doorway at us. 'Wong! What do you think you're doing? In exactly eight minutes you will both be late for dinner.'

'In the Gym – it's Miss – she's—' I spluttered.

'Hazel thinks someone has hurt themselves in the Gym,' said Daisy smoothly. 'She ran back here to get help.'

Virginia scowled in annoyance. 'Oh, honestly,' she said. 'You lot do make up the most corking fibs sometimes.'

'You have to come and look!' I gasped. '*Please!*'

Virginia looked from me to Daisy, and then back to me again. 'If this is one of your games . . .' she warned.

I dragged her back to the Gym with Daisy following. The English mistress, Miss Tennyson, was standing outside Mr MacLean's study at the end of the corridor, talking to sharp-faced, red-haired Mamzelle, the French mistress (I don't know how Miss Tennyson can understand her – Mamzelle has a dreadfully strong French accent; her lessons are a terrible struggle), and grubby old Mr MacLean himself. All three turned and watched us as we went by. In fact, we were making so much noise that The One stuck his head out of his little cubby to see what the fuss was. (The One has his own little office room on the hall end of Library corridor, just next to Mr MacLean's study – he can't use the mistresses' common room at the other end, of course, because he is a man.)

'Problem, Virginia?' Mr MacLean called, and Virginia snapped, 'I *doubt* it, sir.'

As Virginia and Daisy walked through the Gym door, I stopped and clicked the main light switch on triumphantly. 'There she is,' I said, pointing. 'I told you—'

But then I looked down the line of my arm to the place where, a few minutes before, Miss Bell had been lying. Miss Bell was gone. The Gym was quite empty and still. There was only a little dark smear on the polished wooden floor to show where her head had been.

I was still gasping from the shock of it when Virginia spoke.

'Good heavens,' she said. 'What a surprise. There is no one in here. That will be no dinner for either of you tonight – *you*, for lying, and *you* for encouraging her.'

'But she was there!' I cried. 'Honest, she was! Look!' I said, pointing to the dark smear. 'That's *blood*! Somebody must have come back and wiped it up, and—'

Virginia snorted. 'And I'm the Emperor of Japan,' she said in a superior tone of voice. 'They did no such thing, because there never was any body – as you well know. And as for the blood, well, your knee is bleeding. I suppose you thought I wouldn't notice? You've got it on your skirt as well. This is quite one of the most elaborate pieces of nonsense I've ever come across. You really ought to be ashamed – but then, where you come from, I don't suppose they teach you that it's wrong to lie, do they?'

I bit my lip and wished as hard as I could that I had found Virginia Overton lying on the Gym floor.

'Now, come along up to House, both of you. I hope Matron gives you a frightful rollicking for this later, that's all I can say.'

And with that she seized us by the arm and frog-marched us out of the Gym, muttering about useless third formers. I was scarlet with rage and shame. I really *had* seen Miss Bell lying there, I *knew* it – but there was no evidence to show that I hadn't made it all up.

Virginia walked us back past Mamzelle, Miss Tennyson and Mr MacLean. Mamzelle chuckled and said, 'False alarm?'

'Very,' Virginia told her, and kept on walking.

I wondered for a bit if I *were* mad. This sort of thing simply did not happen outside of Daisy's books. It was ridiculous.

But then, as Virginia rushed us out through the bright lights and wood panelling of Old Wing Entrance, I happened to glance down at my skirt and saw the dark stain streaked across it. I opened up the palm of my hand towards me and saw that my index finger still had a faint tidemark of red around its tip. I closed my hand up again into a tight ball, and I knew that I was not mad in the slightest.

5

Even at the furious pace Virginia was pulling us up the hill, we had still not quite reached House when the dinner gong sounded. I flinched automatically when I heard it in the distance, which was my Deepdean training coming out again. One of the first things you learn at Deepdean is that bells are sacred. Our lives are parcelled up into the spaces between one and the next, and to ignore the summons is simply criminal. The most important bell of all is the House dinner gong. If you hear it and do not respond to it, or, worse, if you are not there to hear it at all – well! There will be no dinner for you.

I knew, of course, that we were in much greater trouble than simply missing the dinner gong, but all the same I couldn't help reacting to it.

People were still filing in as we came through the main House doors into the peeling old front hallway, but, 'Wait here!' snapped Virginia, and we were forced to loiter nervously beneath the big hallway clock – which informed us that we were a whole four minutes late – as she went storming upstairs to fetch Matron.

Matron did not look happy to hear what Virginia had to say. Her mean piggy eyes glared at us from beneath her regulation cap, and she breathed heavily through her nose. When Virginia had finished, there was a lull. I could hear the babble from the Dining Room through the closed swing doors. Then Matron came steaming up to us, whacked us both round the head (me harder than Daisy, because after all she had only abetted my lies), and sent us up to our dorm without dinner, to think about what we had done. As we trailed up the scuffed blue carpet of the front stairs I saw Matron going in to dinner with Virginia by her side. They were muttering together and giving us dark backward looks so we would know how out of favour we were.

I was feeling horribly depressed at not being believed. As well as that, thinking about what I had seen in the Gym gave me a nasty taste in my mouth, like the beginning of being sick. Daisy, though, was in very good spirits. As soon as the dorm door swung closed and we were properly alone, she sat down on her bed with a bounce and a crunch (our beds are not supposed to be comfortable), and said, '*Explain.*'

'There's nothing to explain,' I said, sitting down next

to her and feeling sicker than ever. 'I saw Miss Bell lying in the gym. She must have fallen from the balcony. She was absolutely stone cold dead. I didn't make it up!'

'Well, I know you didn't,' said Daisy, as if it was the most natural thing in the world to come across the corpses of Science mistresses in deserted gymnasiums. 'You'd never tell a lie like that. Perhaps Lavinia, but not you. Are you sure she was really dead, though?'

At that, I sat up indignantly, but then I remembered the way Miss Bell's head had lolled and felt sick again. 'I touched her and she was still warm, but dead as anything,' I said. 'She flopped. I told you, she must have fallen off the balcony.'

Daisy sniffed. 'Fallen?'

'What do you mean?' I asked. My skin crawled. I had been so busy being horrified at the fact that Miss Bell was dead that I had not thought properly about how it might have happened.

'It's quite obvious,' said Daisy. 'No one falls to their death and then gets up and tidies *themselves* away, do they? When you first found the body it could have just been an accident. But when we came racing back not five minutes later to find no body at all where one used to be – well. Someone must have pushed her, then got rid of the evidence.'

I gulped. 'Do you mean she's been *murdered?*'

'Yes!' said Daisy. 'Don't tell me you didn't think of

that before? Oh, Hazel, how exciting. A real murder, at Deepdean! Of course, there's always a chance I'm quite wrong. Perhaps you came in just at the wrong moment and misunderstood things—'

'I did not,' I said, annoyed again.

'Or we simply missed the rescue party somehow. Well. If it is that – and how I hope it isn't – we'll know as soon as we get in tomorrow morning. It'll be all over school like the mumps.'

'But if it isn't?' I asked, although I really knew the answer.

'If it isn't,' said Daisy, bouncing on her bed again and beaming at me, 'then our Detective Society has just found our best case yet.'

6

We heard the Dining-Room doors bang open down-stairs. There was a gathering roar and a clatter of feet up the bare sides of the stairs, and thirty seconds later Kitty threw open the dorm door and came rushing in, Beanie and Lavinia at her heels.

'What happened? Why weren't you at dinner?' gasped Beanie. 'I saved you my pudding in case you haven't eaten – it's bakewell tart so it was easy to carry and you *know* I hate it.'

I knew that was a lie, and felt guilty, but before I could argue Daisy had graciously taken the crumbling slice of tart from Beanie and was breaking it in half. It had been wrapped in Beanie's handkerchief, so was not entirely clean, but my stomach was rumbling. It tasted heavenly.

'What happened?' asked Kitty while we were eating.

'What did you do? I must say, Matron and VO were both looking fearfully enraged about something.'

'No change from the usual, then,' said Daisy through a mouthful of tart. 'It was nothing really. Hazel went back to the Gym to get her pullover, and VO caught her in there and decided she was loitering where she oughtn't. We got into awful trouble with her.'

Everyone nodded knowingly. Virginia Overton's rages were legendary.

To divert attention away from the Gym, and in thanks for Beanie's offering, Daisy dug into the contents of her tuck box and came up with a bar of Fry's chocolate. We were all still sitting on our beds munching it when the bell for homework – which we call *Prep* – rang loudly.

That evening, even though I had masses of prep, I couldn't settle down to it at all. I kept on thinking about Miss Bell, and how Daisy and I now knew she had been murdered. For all Daisy's talk, the Wells and Wong Detective Society had never really detected anything more important than very minor theft. But what if we managed to solve this case? We would be heroines. Miss Griffin might give us medals, and the mistresses, the masters and the Big Girls would all line up to clap us on the back – all, of course, apart from the murderer.

That thought brought me back down to earth with a thump. I put down my pen, and King Henry, who was taking Prep that evening, said, 'Come on, Wong, buck up!'

Murders, unfortunately, always come with murderers attached. In Daisy's books, they generally get quite angry about being investigated – and, in fact, dreadful things tend to happen to anyone who knows too much about the crime. I had been there, on the spot, straight after a murder had been committed. What if the murderer had seen me?

~~⟞ PART TWO ⟝~~

WE BEGIN OUR INVESTIGATION

1

The thought kept on worrying me, all the way through Prep. I wanted to slip a note to Daisy about it, but King Henry was glaring at me too hard. What if the murderer had seen me? After all, it must have been a close-run thing to make Miss Bell vanish between the first time I had gone into the Gym and the second.

After we had lined up in the washroom for toothbrushes, three to each porcelain sink, we got into bed. I took advantage of a pillow fight between Kitty and Lavinia to creep over to Daisy's narrow bed and climb in beside her.

'Daisy,' I whispered. 'What if the murderer *saw* me?'

'Saw you do what?' Daisy asked, rolling over. 'Ow, Hazel, your feet are blocks of ice.'

'Saw me in the Gym. After the murder!'

Daisy sighed. 'How on earth would they have seen

33

you? They weren't there when you came in the first time, were they?'

'No,' I said. 'But what if they were hiding? In the Cupboard perhaps?'

'You're a chump,' said Daisy. 'If they were in the Cupboard, they couldn't have *seen* you through the closed door, could they? And you didn't say anything, did you, so even if they *were* hiding they couldn't have known it was you.'

'But we came back! What about then? How do you know for certain that they won't be after us both now that we know?'

'VO didn't say our names,' said Daisy wearily. 'I'm sure she didn't. Therefore the murderer will have no idea who either of us is. I promise you, Hazel, on my word as an excellent detective. Say it. I am an excellent detective.'

'You are an excellent detective,' I said, because she was digging her fingers into my arm.

'You see? It's quite all right. There's nothing to be worried about.'

I tried to make myself believe her.

'Unless, of course,' said Daisy casually, 'the murderer is just biding their time; waiting to find out exactly who we are and how much we saw before they come after us both. But that's not particularly likely. Now go back to your own bed, Watson, you're squashing me. We've got important work to do tomorrow.'

I went back to my bed, but it was a very long time before I got to sleep. I could hear Daisy breathing peacefully next to me, and thumping from Lavinia's bed as she rolled to and fro in her sleep. But then there were other noises I was not so sure about. The House pipes squealed and groaned louder than I had ever heard them before, and then there was a squeak below me, rattles and rustles in the walls; a soft sigh just outside the door. A floorboard, I told myself – mice . . . Matron on her rounds – but I was most shamefully afraid. I squeezed my eyes tight shut, to stop myself looking at the curtain floating in the breeze from our open window (Matron believes that fresh air is good for children), and tried to be brave. But I kept seeing Miss Bell's head lolling away from me, and when I did get to sleep my dreams were awful.

2

We began our detective work the next day.

We filed into Prayers, The One blaring away at the organ, to find that Miss Bell was not in her usual seat. This was just as Daisy and I expected, of course, but shocking for the rest of the school. You see, Miss Bell had never been late for anything before. She had always been perfectly punctual, so her absence from Prayers seemed as impossible as the Hall simply falling down around our heads. The wooden pews filled, and although the rule in Prayers is dead silence, punishable by detention, a whisper rose up like a shell pressed against your ear, making all the mistresses and prefects frown and glare about them.

'Where's Miss Bell?' breathed Beanie. 'She's *never* ill!'

'Perhaps this is the day Miss Griffin is going to announce that she's the new Deputy,' Kitty whispered back, louder than she meant to. 'I'll bet anything they're about to come onto the stage together.'

'Girls!' snarled Mamzelle, whipping round from the row in front to glare at the third form. Her sharp face was looking particularly sour, and we quietened down at once. '*Silence*. Contemplate 'eaven, eef you please.'

The third form was quiet. But then Miss Griffin walked onto the stage, making us all rise to our feet, and she was alone. Kitty nudged Beanie in amazement, but then Miss Griffin began to speak and it was impossible not to pay attention to what she was saying.

I have not yet said much about Miss Griffin, other than that she is our Headmistress. That is because it is quite difficult to remember that Miss Griffin might need describing. Miss Griffin is a presence. I cannot imagine Deepdean without Miss Griffin, or Miss Griffin without Deepdean. If the school was a person, it would wear Miss Griffin's neat swooped-back grey hair and immaculate Harris tweed.

Every day she glides along the corridors in sensible shoes that are just high enough to click. When I heard her during lessons I used to vaguely connect her with an automaton from the future. Even though I know it is shrimp-like foolishness, I still rather think that if you peeled away Miss Griffin's tidy outside you would find rows of gleaming clockwork wheels, busily ticking over to keep Deepdean going. It is very difficult to have an emotion about her, the way I like Mamzelle (despite her incomprehensible accent) and despise hockey-playing Miss Hopkins. Miss Griffin is simply *there*, as much a part of Deepdean School as the building itself. You only ever get to know her if you are one of the particularly promising Big Girls, whom she tutors for university entrance exams, or a prefect – who are not at all like the rest of us.

Miss Griffin gave her sermon, all about honour and striving which are the themes most Tuesdays. As soon as she began to run through the daily messages, you could feel the whole school waiting to hear news about Miss Bell, but there was only a reminder about the fourth form's visit to a museum next Wednesday and then a scolding little notice about mess in The One's art room.

It may seem a bit odd, since Miss Griffin did not say anything at all about Miss Bell, but that was how I *knew* that she had been murdered. If even Miss Griffin did not know what had happened to Miss Bell, then the murderer really had managed to hide what they had done. Just as Daisy had said, it was up to us to detect it. The Detective Society's first real case! My stomach jumped like one of Lavinia's Mexican beans, and I couldn't tell whether I was terrified or wildly excited.

Miss Griffin, of course, had no idea about the state of my insides. 'And now, the hymn,' she said.

It was 'Lift Up Your Hearts'. The One pounded away with gusto, and under cover of the organ's enormous trumpeting blares Daisy leaned over to me.

'*E'en so, with one accord* – so, nothing about the Bell, then,' she sang.

'I know – *we lift them to the Lord*,' I replied. 'What shall we do?'

'Detect, of course,' warbled Daisy. 'We'll talk about our first lines of enquiry later – *The mire of sin, the weight of guilty fears* – isn't this song apt, though!'

Miss Griffin glared out from her podium, as though she had heard us, and I gulped and went back to singing the proper words.

3

It seemed that the masters and mistresses were determined to carry on as though nothing had changed. I wondered who would be waiting for us when we arrived for Science in second hour, but even I was amazed when we found Mamzelle waiting in Miss Bell's usual place, with a white lab coat on over her silky blouse. The rest of the form were simply gobsmacked.

'Bonjour, girls,' Mamzelle said. 'Mees Bell eez not 'ere *aujourd'hui, et alors* I will be taking you for ze lesson.'

'Will we have to speak in French?' asked Beanie in consternation.

'Not unless you want to, Rebecca,' said Mamzelle, shaking her hair and pursing her lips in amusement. 'Fear not, in *la France* I was ze mistress for Science, and so I know about what I will be teaching.'

'What's happened to Miss Bell?' asked Kitty.

'I cannot tell you Mees Bell's business, Kitty. I can only say that she eez not in school today and so I must take her lessons for her. Now sit down, all of you, and we will discuss ze cells of plants, which I gather eez what Mees Bell had planned for you.'

'Curiouser and curiouser,' whispered Daisy to me as we sat down. I could see everyone else around the room making surprised faces at each other behind their textbooks.

I really did feel as though I had fallen down Alice's rabbit hole. Even if I had not seen Miss Bell lying there on the Gym floor, I would have known that something terrible had happened to her. Miss Bell, after all, had never been even a minute late for a single lesson, and now here she was, missing an entire morning of school. If I had been a master or mistress, I would have been ringing for the police directly, but it seemed none of them had. It was infuriating.

I was itching to speak to Daisy about it, and I could see, from the way that she was bouncing about on her chair, that she was dying to talk to me as well.

The bell for bunbreak rang, and Daisy spun round to face me. 'All right, Watson, this is it! Mental casebook at the ready! Our first mission is to dig up all the idle gossip we can. Before we begin our investigation properly, I want to know what everyone *else* thinks is going on.'

I would have preferred to proceed straight to the investigation, but there is no use arguing with Daisy when she has a Detective Society mission in mind. So I summoned all my Watson-y thoughts, nodded, and followed her outside.

4

On the lawn, the whole school was buzzing with made-up news about Miss Bell. Unfortunately, none of it suggested that she might be dead. On the contrary, most people seemed to think she had decided to run away – generally because she had been jilted by The One, although there were odder theories. One of the shrimps was telling us that Miss Bell was on the run because the government was after her, (although the shrimp could not say why the government might be interested in a schoolmistress), and another shrimp insisted that it was not the government at all, but a secret organization that had something to do with *the East*. She looked at me rather fearfully as she said that, as though being from Hong Kong made me the East in human form and therefore untrustworthy. I hate all that. Usually, once they know me, English people simply pretend that I am not Oriental, and I simply do not remind them about it. But sometimes they slip, and little bits of nastiness that are usually hidden come sliding out of their mouths, which can be quite difficult to politely ignore.

That particular bunbreak I was doomed to have my difference noticed. I had several people hurriedly stop talking when we wandered past their groups, presumably in case I was a hostile agent of the East. Then a fifth former whom I had never spoken to before came up to ask me if it was really true that my father ran the opium trade. My father is a banker in Hong Kong, and I told her so. It was plain that she did not believe me.

'She needn't be snobbish about it,' said Daisy to me when the fifth former had run off to join her friends. 'Her father's a dastardly smuggler. Everyone knows that.'

I was comforted by this, although I never quite know where Daisy gets this sort of information from. She is always coming out with things like that, but when I asked her once she only said, 'Oh, you know, my uncle,' and looked vague.

After that Daisy vanished into the crowd of people eating their buns on the North Lawn. She was gone some time. I craned my head around looking for her, but then someone seized the back of my pullover and I turned round to see Daisy again, looking very cheerful.

'Listen to this!' she hissed. 'The rumour is that

Miss Bell's resigned. I just spoke to King Henry, and she told me.'

It might sound odd – that a third former like Daisy should be able to speak to the lofty Head Girl – but it is merely another absolutely English thing. The English have a habit of being related to nearly anyone you can mention, and King Henry turns out to be the fifth cousin of Daisy's mother. She and Daisy go riding together in the hols and have tea visits and so on, which makes it all right for Daisy to talk to King Henry sometimes when they are at Deepdean.

'There was a letter on the Headmistress's desk this morning; King Henry read it because Miss Griffin showed her. Miss Griffin is still trying to decide the right time to break it to the girls. King Henry must have liked Miss Bell more than I thought: she was looking awfully distressed when she told me.'

'But Miss Bell can't have resigned!' I exclaimed.

'I know *that*,' said Daisy irritably. 'Miss Bell's stone dead and therefore incapable of writing anything, let alone a resignation letter. But don't you see what this means? It absolutely proves, once and for all, that what you discovered was a murder; and that the murderer is someone who knows Miss Bell's handwriting well enough to forge it. It's also got to be someone high up enough in the school to be able to march into Miss Griffin's office and plant the letter on her desk.'

'A master or mistress!' I gasped, horrified. '*That's* why they're all pretending that nothing's wrong!'

'Well, not all of them did it,' Daisy pointed out. 'But the one who did – whoever it was – has managed to bamboozle the others with that note. That's what Mamzelle meant about not "prying into Miss Bell's affairs". This is really it, Hazel. This means that it's up to us! If the Detective Society doesn't do something, nobody will!'

I had a momentary un-detective-like pang. 'Are you sure we shouldn't just go to the police?' I asked.

'Don't be stupid,' said Daisy severely. 'We don't have any evidence yet. We don't even have a body. They'd simply laugh at us. No, we're on our own. And anyway, this is *our* murder case.'

I was not sure I liked the sound of that. Daisy was talking as though the case was just another tuck theft, but I knew it wasn't. What I had seen in the Gym had become, in my mind, my own personal ghost story in which bodies appeared and then vanished into thin air. Except that it wasn't a story at all, but very real. I was still terrified at the thought that the murderer might know that I had seen Miss Bell's body. What if I ended up a corpse myself? In a few years it might be *my* bloody ghost that all the Big Girls frightened the shrimps with, instead of Verity Abraham's. The thought made me shudder.

'But I thought you didn't even *like* Miss Bell,' I said, to make myself stop thinking about it.

'It's not about liking,' said Daisy sternly. 'It's the principle of the thing. People can't be allowed to get away with murder at Deepdean. Oh Hazel, it'll be so exciting! The Detective Society will be real at last!'

At this point, the bell rang for the end of bunbreak.

'Right,' said Daisy. 'I move for our first official meeting to be held after Prep this evening. In the meantime, since the murder of Miss Bell is now a proper Wells and Wong Detective Society case, you can keep on writing up notes, and I'll start planning our course of action. And we can both keep our eyes and ears open. Detective Society handshake?'

We shook hands, clicked our fingers, shook again, made the Mystery Gesture, and then rushed off for Art with The One.

5

I gave up on the rest of Tuesday's lessons. I spent all my lunch break scribbling case notes, and then tucked this casebook into my French textbook and carried on writing. Daisy, sitting next to me, covered for me beautifully (and only nudged me when she didn't agree with what I was writing). She was stewing away at the problem too.

Usually Daisy takes care to dawdle over her prep, and sigh, and look puzzled, and pass notes to people about the second part of question four. That evening, though, she flew through it and then sat gazing raptly at a chip of paint on the wall until Virginia Overton who, unluckily for us, was taking Prep that evening, snapped, 'Wells! Nose back in your book.'

After that, Daisy bent her head over her exercise book and spent the next fifteen minutes pretending to write. On my other side, Beanie was stuck in the tortures of her French assignment, her face screwed up and the end of her plait jammed into her mouth. Beyond her, Lavinia was plodding angrily through a Latin exercise. From behind us, Kitty kicked Beanie's chair and passed up a note. Beanie looked at it and squeaked with laughter, and the noise made Virginia look up – just in time to see Daisy slip a folded up piece of paper onto my desk.

'Wells!' said Virginia. '*No passing notes*, you know the rules. If it's so important, you can jolly well come up here and read it out to all of us.'

Daisy did not look alarmed by this at all. She stood up, took the paper back from me and walked to the front of the prep room. At Virginia's desk she turned to face us all, opened up the piece of paper and, in a solemn voice, read out, '*I wish Cook would give us something other than sprouts for dinner; they disagree with me awfully.*'

'Wells, you little beast!' cried Virginia as we all squealed with laughter. 'Give that to me!'

She snatched the page from Daisy's hand and read it through, her face flushing with annoyance. 'Oh, go and sit down, and if I hear anything more from you this evening I shall report you to Matron. And be quiet, the rest of you little horrors! Shush! *Shush!*'

Daisy, triumphant, gave her audience the slightest of curtseys and then took her seat again amidst general delighted chaos and furious shushings from Virginia.

As she sank down next to me, though, she leaned her head against mine for a moment and whispered, 'Meeting in the airing cupboard tonight after toothbrushes to talk about you-know-what.'

I went back to pretending to write an essay on the failings of George III. Classic Daisy, I thought. It was just like her. Then my stomach squished as I thought about what she had just said. Were we really ready for our first murder case?

6

Later, when all the prefects on duty were running about chasing shrimps who should have already been in bed (there were a great deal more of them than usual that evening, and I suspect that Daisy may have been behind it), I slipped out – with my casebook stuffed up my pyjama jacket and clutching my toothbrush for cover – and tiptoed down to the airing cupboard on the second-floor corridor. A moment later Daisy padded into view, in her slippers and regulation pyjamas, looking extremely casual. She peered up and down the dim corridor, then, satisfied that there was no one else in sight, seized my arm, more or less dragged me into the airing cupboard and pulled the door shut behind her.

The air inside was thick and damp and very dark – I stumbled against Daisy and she said, 'Ow, Hazel, you clod.'

There was a ripping noise and a snap, which made me jump. I said, 'What's that?' and Daisy said, 'Our cover. Oh, do stop flailing about . . . Here—'

With a *pop* the electric light came on.

Rows and rows of wooden racks piled with grey school clothes came into view, as did Daisy, who was leaning back against the racks and glaring at me. I saw that one of the buttons on her pyjama jacket had been ripped off, leaving the fabric poking through.

'Well,' said Daisy, 'sit down.'

I perched myself on a grey pile of games knickers. This made the wooden slats of the shelf creak danger-ously, and I jumped off again.

'All right,' said Daisy, leaping up onto a rack with a cheerful bounce, and swinging her slippered feet as she spoke. 'This meeting of the Detective Society is hereby called into session at ten minutes past eight on this, Tuesday the thirtieth of October. Present are Daisy Wells, President, and Hazel Wong, Secretary. Tonight we will be discussing the Case of the Murder of Miss Bell. Any objections?'

'No,' I said, writing busily.

'Excellent, Watson,' said Daisy. 'All right, the order of the meeting is as follows: first, the facts of the case. Second, the suspect list. Third, the current location of the body. And fourth, our plan of action.'

'Do we *have* any facts of the case?' I asked, pausing

and looking up at Daisy. It seemed to me that we were starting off without any of the things that detectives usually take for granted. The body had vanished (and even though I had seen it, I had been too busy behaving like a frightened little shrimp to pay proper attention to it), and what was left of the crime scene must by now have been tidied away by Jones the handyman on his rounds. We had no photographic snaps to look at, no police interviews to read and no coroner's report to look at either. To me, the situation seemed rather bleak.

'Of course we do!' said Daisy. 'Come on, Hazel, don't give up before we've even started. We know there was a murder because you found the body. We know *who* was murdered – Miss Bell – and how she was murdered too.'

'By being pushed off the Gym balcony!' I agreed.

'We can also make a jolly good stab at *when* it happened. Look – the last lesson of the day ends at four fifteen p.m. – which on Mondays happens to be second-form Dance. You went to the Gym—?'

'At five forty-five,' I said.

'That means that Miss Bell must have been killed some time between four fifteen – after all, one of those second formers would have noticed the body if it was there during Dance – and five forty-five. There, you see? That's *what, who*, where *how* and *when*. That wasn't so difficult.'

I realized she was right.

'So, we do have some facts after all,' Daisy went on. 'And that brings us rather neatly to our second point: the suspects. Who might want to do away with Miss Bell – or rather, considering what's happened this term, who wouldn't?'

'Do you really think it has to be a master or mistress?' I asked.

'I think what we've worked out already practically proves it,' said Daisy. 'The resignation note, left on Miss Griffin's desk, in handwriting that looked like Miss Bell's – only a master or mistress could have done that, after all. And we've worked out that Miss Bell was killed after school hours, by someone strong enough to shove her over the side of the Gym balcony. I'd say that was all quite conclusive. So, which of them could have done it?'

'Well, Miss Parker,' I said. 'Because of what happened with Miss Bell and The One.'

'The jealousy angle,' said Daisy. 'I like it. Think of all those rows they've been having!'

I thought about Miss Parker in one of her legendary rages, dragging her fingers through her short black hair and shrieking, and decided that she was a very good suspect indeed.

'Who else?' Daisy asked.

'What about Miss Hopkins? She might have been afraid The One would jilt her for Miss Bell.'

'Now, that's a silly suggestion,' said Daisy. 'For one thing, it's a terribly weak motive. For another, I happen to know that Miss Hopkins was up in the Pavilion talking tactics with the hockey lot on Monday after school. They've got that match against St Chator's this weekend, you know – they're terrified about it, so the Hop was helping them prepare. She couldn't have killed Miss Bell. And for a third – well, Miss Hopkins simply wouldn't do a thing like murder. She couldn't. She's – she's *pukka*.'

It was my turn to sigh. Daisy is quite obsessed with Miss Hopkins, and I felt that she was ruling her out unfairly. But I couldn't argue with such an alibi.

'All right, then,' I said. 'Miss Lappet and Miss Tennyson. They both want the Deputy Head job, don't they, but we all know that Miss Bell was about to be given it. What if one of them thought they'd get it by clearing Miss Bell out of the way?'

'*Much* better,' said Daisy, pleased. 'Neither of them have alibis that I can think of – and we know that Miss Tennyson was around school at the right time, don't we? After all, she took us for Lit. Soc yesterday, and societies all finish at five twenty. And then we saw her outside Mr MacLean's study shortly after you discovered the body, not far from the Gym at all. So . . . who else? I suppose Mamzelle and Mr MacLean, because we saw them near the scene of the crime at the right time too. Though I can't think of a motive for either of them, can you?'

I shook my head. 'Shouldn't we add The One, for the same reason?' I asked. 'He was there – I saw him stick his head out of his cubby as we were going past.'

'Very true,' agreed Daisy, nodding. 'Though, again, why ever would he kill Miss Bell? It's not as though he's even interested in her any more. Really, it ought to have been *her* killing *him*, and of course that didn't happen.'

'Rage?' I suggested. 'Blackmail? Remorse?'

'Hmm,' said Daisy. 'Not yet proven. But lovely work otherwise. Just look, we've got six suspects for our list! Write them down, do. Then we can cross them off later as we discover their alibis.'

I wrote them down.

SUSPECT LIST

1. *Miss Parker.* MOTIVE: Jealous rage. ALIBI: None yet.

2. ~~*Miss Hopkins.* MOTIVE: Getting rid of a love rival. ALIBI: Good. Up in Pavilion at time of murder.~~ RULED OUT.

3. *Miss Lappet.* MOTIVE: Wants the Deputy Headmistress job. ALIBI: None yet.

4. *Miss Tennyson*. MOTIVE: Wants the Deputy Headmistress job. ALIBI: None yet. NOTES: Was observed near Gym just after murder, by Daisy Wells and Hazel Wong.

5. *Mamzelle*. MOTIVE: None yet. ALIBI: None yet. NOTES: Was observed near Gym just after murder, by Daisy Wells and Hazel Wong.

6. *Mr MacLean*. MOTIVE: None yet. ALIBI: None yet. NOTES: Was observed near Gym just after murder, by Daisy Wells and Hazel Wong.

7. *The One*. MOTIVE: ~~Anger? Blackmail?~~ None yet. ALIBI: None yet. NOTES: Was observed near Gym just after murder, by Daisy Wells and Hazel Wong.

'All right, excellent work,' said Daisy. 'Now we must consider the matter of the body.'

I did not like the sound of that at all. In fact, it gave me the shudders. There we were, back again to the horrible idea that the murderer might still have been in the Gym when I arrived.

'Where did it go?' asked Daisy, not noticing the look on my face. 'How did the murderer move it? They wouldn't have had long, after all. If you left the Gym at five forty-five and came back with me and Virginia at, well, let's say five fifty-two – that seems about right – then they wouldn't have been able to get far. Bodies are extraordinarily heavy, my uncle says.'

I wished Daisy hadn't said that. It might have been a joke, but it made my chills worse than ever.

'I'd say that it was more than possible that your suggestion about the murderer hiding in the Cupboard is correct,' said Daisy excitedly, sounding more and more like something from one of her detective novels. 'And he or she could have dragged the body in there too! Imagine – you, me and Virginia, just a few steps away from the killer and the victim. But if it *was* there at that moment, where was it moved to afterwards? Since no one using the Gym today noticed a body, it must have been moved somewhere else after we left yesterday evening. Perhaps the murderer used the trolley that Jones stores in the Cupboard, to move it more easily. Anyway, that's another of our tasks, to discover the current location of Miss Bell's body.'

'Ugh,' I said, shivering. I didn't want to see Miss Bell's corpse ever again, and I couldn't bear the thought that both it and the murderer might have been nearby when I returned to the Gym with Virginia and Daisy. Daisy, however, rolled her eyes at me. Things like that do not bother her at all. I don't think she sees them in her imagination in quite the same way I do.

'I think investigating the body's whereabouts will involve more careful planning than we can manage right now. We can't just go nosing about the school looking for a corpse, after all. I'll have to think about that. But – Hazel, write this down – the plan for tomorrow is as follows: we must establish alibis for the masters and mistresses on our suspect list. We can try asking them directly, of course, but it may be easier simply to ask other girls. However, remember that this mission requires constant vigilance! Any answer may lead to the truth.'

'Yes,' I said, fighting down my nerves. 'I know. But – I still can't believe that one of *our* masters or mistresses could have committed a *murder*.'

'Oh, don't be silly, Hazel. My uncle says anyone's capable of murder, deep down. Only remember—'

But at that moment, the door to the airing cupboard was wrenched open and Virginia Overton appeared before us, looking grim. As quickly as I could, I dropped my casebook onto the floor and sat on it. Luckily, Virginia is sometimes less than observant.

'Whatever are you doing?' she asked us furiously. 'Come out of there at once.'

Daisy was unperturbed. 'The button just popped off my pyjama jacket. Hazel was helping me find a new one.'

'I *don't* think so,' said Virginia. 'It's nearly ten o'clock – you ought to have been in bed half an hour ago. Get back to your dorm immediately, and I shall be telling Matron about this later.'

Under her baleful eye we scurried out of the cupboard towards our dorm, Daisy clutching a new pyjama jacket. 'Beast,' she said, as soon as we were round the corner. 'She only wants us out of it so she and Belinda Vance can canoodle in there. Betsy North says she caught them at it last week.'

'Oh,' I said.

'The problem with this place,' said Daisy, pausing in the stairwell to wriggle out of her old pyjama jacket and into her new one, 'is that there are far too many secrets wherever you turn. And most of them are so *pointless*. It doesn't make it easy for two detectives to do their jobs.'

7

It might seem strange that someone as popular as Daisy should have a secret like the Detective Society. Certainly, when I first met her I never suspected the sort of person she really is. The first time I met Daisy would be hard to forget. It was the first time I'd ever stepped onto a games field – and incidentally, also the first time I truly thought I might die.

I had been at Deepdean for less than a day. My boat from Hong Kong had only docked in England a week before, and I still couldn't understand how anywhere in the world could be so cold. I watched the English girls happily running out onto the field wearing skimpy games skirts, and decided that I would have nothing to do with such madness. But I found myself ordered outside anyway, my lumpy legs sticking out underneath my itchy grey games skirt and games knickers (according to the English, the only place you can get cold is your behind, so they make you put on extra underwear over your real underwear to keep warm), and my frozen pink hands clutching my shiny new hockey stick.

Then Miss Hopkins blew her whistle, and suddenly all the other girls began to pound up and down in front of me, screaming and waving their sticks about as though they wanted to murder each other. It began to rain – not at all like the warm rain I was used to at home, but as though someone was shooting flakes of ice into my face and all up my bare, goose-pimply legs.

That was the moment when I realized that England might not be exactly how it had seemed in my jolly school-story books.

I had been hearing about England – and the boarding schools real English children went to – all my life. My father had studied at one when he was a little boy, and he never stops talking about it. He made me learn to read and write in English – and not only me but all our servants, even the *mui jai* – and then he gave me heaps and heaps of English books to read.

All the same, I never thought I would go to an English school myself. All the boys from families like mine did, of course, but girls generally stayed on Hong Kong Island. I would have too, if two things had not happened: first, my father's concubine had another daughter. This meant that my father's dream of sending a son of his to school in England was ruined again.

Secondly, a girl my family knows, Victoria Cheng, was sent away to Hampden School for Ladies, in Cairo. Her father showed mine a picture of Victoria standing stiffly next to lots of other pale little girls in pinafores, and my father decided on the spot that if the Chengs could do it, we could do it too, and better.

The next thing I knew, my father was telling me that even though it was the middle of the year, I was going away to school myself – and not to Cairo, but to the real thing in England. 'If Cheng thinks that he can get the better of me like that,' said my father, 'he's wrong. Besides, no school in the world could change the fact that his daughter is stupid. My clever Hazel is worth ten Victoria Chengs, and now she's going to prove it.'

My mother was furious. She hates my father's obsession with England. 'Western school never did any Chinese person good,' she said.

'Oh, come now, Lin darling,' said my father, laughing. 'What about me?'

'Exactly,' snapped my mother, and for the next week she refused to speak anything but Cantonese in protest.

Of course, I was wild with excitement. Like my father, I was obsessed with the real, original England. Our big white cake of a house, and the whole compound it sits in, is filled with Western things. We have a tidy green lawn bordered with pink roses (my mother is always complaining about all the watering they need), the Folio Society sends us heavy, beautiful-smelling parcels of books each month to fill up my father's library, and in every room the patterned wallpaper is nearly hidden by paintings – of grand English mansions surrounded by large fields and very small farmers, of people riding beautiful brown horses or taking tea on green lawns. In the dining room we have a great big picture of the King wearing his moustache and medals, next to the Queen with her pearls and white dress. 'It's my little corner of England,' says my father – and when I looked out over the top of our compound wall, at the rickshaw drivers in the loud, dusty streets below, and beyond to Victoria Harbour, jam-packed with its junks and steamers, our house seemed part of a different world entirely.

The day I found out I was going to England I sat in our drawing room – its mahogany furniture a little warped and fuzzy from the heat, its wallpaper peeling – and imagined myself at school, arm-in-arm with a golden-haired girl, a friend who would turn me into a perfect English Miss, like her.

But standing on the cold games field that morning, it seemed to me that all the English Misses were actually horrible and mad. I clutched my hockey stick harder than ever – and then someone ran into me, extremely hard. I wobbled and gasped (I am so solid that it is not easy to knock me over) and the someone said, 'Oh, I say, I'm so very sorry.'

And that, of course, was Daisy. Her hair was falling out of its plaits chaotically and her eyes were extremely blue, and although the rest of England was not exactly turning out as I had expected, here, at least, was one English ideal – my golden-haired friend come to life; a person absolutely made from the England of my books and paintings.

When I think back to that moment, I realize how silly I was.

PART THREE

WE LEARN SOME INTERESTING THINGS

1

On Wednesday morning, Miss Bell was (of course) still missing, and everyone was still very excited about the idea of a gang from the East. Lallie Thompson-Bates, a day girl from the second form, was telling anyone who would listen that her mother had spoken to a close friend who had seen a woman looking very much like Miss Bell in a shop in Abingdon, buying azaleas. Another girl who knew all about the language of flowers said that azaleas meant 'Take care!', and there was great excitement at that – until Lallie admitted that she had meant to say hydrangeas. Since hydrangeas turned out to mean 'frigidity', this did not seem right at all.

'And I don't know when she would have time for buying flowers if she was really on the run from a criminal gang,' Daisy whispered to me scornfully, before turning to Kitty to discuss whether the people after Miss Bell might perhaps be from Russia.

Daisy cultivates girls in the lower forms to bring her back gossip, and so she sent Betsy North and her other informants off to collect information, telling them quite truthfully that she wanted to know what Miss Bell had been doing on Monday before her mysterious disappearance. She and I canvassed the older girls.

We discovered that, while it was difficult to stop people talking about Miss Bell, most of the things they said were utterly useless. But then Betsy came back to us with some much more useful news.

One of Betsy's little first-form friends had been to Cultural Soc on Monday with Mamzelle. This was useful already, since it reminded us that Mamzelle had a good alibi between 4.20 and 5.20, but then the story became even more interesting. The shrimp had been let out of Cultural Soc five minutes early because she had a slight stomach ache. At just after 5.15 she had arrived in Old Wing cloakroom to collect her hat and coat, and there she had unexpectedly come upon Miss Bell. Miss Bell was, according to the shrimp, digging through a pile of old coats; then she pulled out a battered copy of *The Arabian Nights*, snapped, 'I'm confiscating this,' and stalked off towards Library corridor.

Daisy and I both realized what this meant at once. It brought the time during which the killer must have struck down to less than half an hour. If Miss Bell had been alive and in Old Wing cloakroom at 5.15, she could not have even arrived in the Gym before 5.20, and that meant she must have been killed between 5.20 and 5.45.

'Do you know,' said Daisy to me, once Betsy had run off again, 'detecting a murder is turning out to be rather easy. If we carry on like this we shall have solved it in no time.'

I was not so sure. It seemed to me that we still had a great deal to discover. But I did agree that we seemed to be making a very good start, and soon we had even more information.

A fourth former waiting about for confirmation study with Mr MacLean had seen Miss Bell go into the mistresses' common room on Library corridor, just after lessons ended but before socs began, followed by Miss Parker. A few minutes later they had come out again – both looking frightfully cross, Miss Bell's face icy and Miss Parker's hair all spiky with rage (the fourth former's words) – and marched away together towards an empty form room. This sounded very much like the beginnings of another spectacular argument. That it had taken place on the evening Miss Bell died was extremely suspicious.

Then Felicity Carrington (a fifth former, who was dreadfully disappointed that she had nothing to say about Miss Bell) mentioned that she had seen Miss Lappet going into Miss Griffin's office just after half past four, her glasses wobbling and her enormous bosom heaving, looking terribly upset about something. Daisy was very excited. 'What if she was complaining about Miss Bell being given the Deputy job?' she asked me in a low voice. 'And then, if Miss Griffin refused to listen to her, what if she decided to take matters into *her own hands*?'

'Hmm,' I said thoughtfully. We now knew that two more of our suspects had stayed at school after hours, and neither of them yet had any sort of alibi for the time of the murder. I noted it all down on our suspect list.

2

Things began to look very black for Miss Parker. In Maths, Daisy began talking loudly about a favourite fountain pen that she must have lost somewhere in the corridors after Lit. Soc on Monday evening. '*You* didn't see it, did you?' she asked Miss Parker.

'You mustn't be so careless with your possessions,' Miss Parker told her crossly while she scribbled scarlet correction lines across her work. 'You are a wickedly negligent girl sometimes. As it happens, I left school at the end of lessons on Monday, so I wouldn't have come across it.'

She turned to give Beanie a telling off (she was gnawing her plait and staring despairingly at a page so covered in scored out numbers it was almost solid blue), and I spun round to Daisy in excitement. Kitty, however, got there first. She nudged Daisy, grinning.

'Gosh, what a filthy liar she is!' she whispered,

glancing carefully over at Miss Parker, who was now shouting at Beanie. 'What she said about leaving at the end of school's a load of tosh. I saw her when I was walking back towards Library corridor after Cultural Soc ended. She was sitting in one of the empty form rooms, her face all angry scarlet. And her hair was in such a state! I'd bet anything that she and Miss Bell had been arguing again— I say! I wonder if she's a secret agent for this Russian crime ring that's kidnapped Miss Bell! Wouldn't that be exciting?'

'Hum,' said Daisy, looking across the room. 'If I were a Russian crime lord and wanted a secret agent' – Miss Parker was holding her head in her hands and groaning in frustration as Beanie gave her a fifth wrong answer to the same question – 'I wouldn't choose *Miss Parker*. She'd refuse to do anything and then run off in a rage.'

'Very true,' said Kitty, and giggled.

I nudged Daisy, extremely impressed by her evasive tactics, and she winked back at me. We both knew that we were getting somewhere. Miss Parker's alibi was becoming weaker and weaker – we now knew that she had been near the Gym, alone, close to the time when Miss Bell's murder must have taken place, and she had lied about it. Had she really argued with Miss Bell again? If so, why was she trying to hide it? It was like a plot from one of Daisy's books.

But all the same, I couldn't help wondering whether

Miss Parker could really *kill* someone. She was a very angry person, and we all knew it – but so is Lavinia, and for all her shouting she is really mostly harmless. It's as if all that yelling and kicking gets the rage out of her and she has none left to do worse things. Was it the same for Miss Parker?

'But what if *Mamzelle* was the kidnapper?' asked Kitty as we were walking between lessons. Evidently she was still thinking about what Daisy had said in Maths; about secret Russian agents abducting Miss Bell. 'She's been behaving awfully strangely lately – Sophie, tell them what you told me yesterday.'

Sophie Croke-Finchley, who is in the other third form dorm and is a musical prodigy, grinned. 'Oh yes,' she said. 'It was terribly odd. I had my lesson with The One—'

'When?' asked Daisy, cutting her off.

'Oh, four twenty to four fifty, same as always,' Sophie said, blinking a bit. 'But *anyway*, I stayed on in the Music room afterwards, practising, and I noticed after a bit that someone else was in the small practice room next to me, and they were making the oddest sounds. Garglings and yellings – not music at all! I thought for a while that there were two people in there, speaking in tongues, but then I realized that it was Mamzelle, talking to herself in English and then repeating it in French! She carried on for ages – until almost five forty-five, when I had to go – and then just as I was leaving she came out of her practice room, and saw me. She looked awfully frightened, for some reason, and then she hared down the hall towards New Wing. Isn't that odd?'

Daisy and I agreed that it was. But all I could think was how we finally had a proper alibi for one of our suspects.

3

In Div., we found another alibi.

Mr MacLean, who we had seen lurking so promisingly next to the Gym on Monday evening, certainly looks a bit like a murderer. He wears filthy, egg-stained jackets, his hair is greasy, and in Prayers he leers at us over the lectern. It would have been very easy and satisfying if he had been Miss Bell's killer, but it was not to be. Mr MacLean began telling us all about the confirmation training we would be taking next year, when we got to the fourth form. 'The girls enjoy it so!' he said, beaming at us with his nasty yellow teeth. 'Why, the class I took on Monday was so fascinating that we managed to overrun by nearly half an hour! In the end I had to tell them to hurry so as not to be late for dinner!'

If that was true, it gave Mr MacLean an alibi for the time of the murder. When we got back up to House for lunch, Daisy made enquiries – and Mr MacLean's impossibly perfect alibi turned out to be entirely true. He had let his class out at 5.45, which meant that he would not have been able to go to the Gym, murder Miss Bell and be back in Library corridor talking to Mamzelle and Miss Tennyson by the time we saw him there on Monday evening.

Daisy and I looked at each other in amazement. We had managed to get rid of two suspects in one morning.

It was time to update my suspect list.

SUSPECT LIST

1. *Miss Parker.* MOTIVE: Jealous rage.
   ALIBI: None yet between 5.20 and 5.45p.m.
   NOTES: Was seen arguing with the victim
   at 4.20 on the day of the murder and at 5.20
   observed alone in New Wing form room (near
   Gym) by Kitty Freebody.

2. ~~*Miss Hopkins.* MOTIVE: Getting rid
   of a love rival. ALIBI: Good. Up in Pavilion at
   time of murder.~~ RULED OUT.

3. *Miss Lappet.* MOTIVE: Wants the Deputy Headmistress job. ALIBI: None yet. NOTES: Was seen going into Miss Griffin's study just after 4.30, in agitated state, by Felicity Carrington.

4. *Miss Tennyson.* MOTIVE: Wants the Deputy Headmistress job. ALIBI: None yet between 5.20 and 5.50. NOTES: Was observed near Gym just after murder, by Daisy Wells and Hazel Wong.

5. *Mamzelle.* ~~MOTIVE: None yet. ALIBI: (None yet.) Good. In Music Wing between 5.20 and 5.45, observed by Sophie Croke-Finchley. NOTES: Was observed near Gym just after murder, by Daisy Wells and Hazel Wong.~~ RULED OUT.

6. *Mr MacLean.* ~~MOTIVE: None yet. ALIBI: (None yet.) Good. In study with class of confirmation students between 5.20 and 5.45. NOTES: Was observed near Gym just after murder, by Daisy Wells and Hazel Wong.~~ RULED OUT.

7. *The One.* MOTIVE: ~~Anger? Blackmail?~~
None yet. ALIBI: ~~None yet.~~ Taking Sophie
Croke-Finchley for Music lesson between 4.20
and 4.50 but none yet between 5.20 and 5.45.
NOTES: Was observed near Gym just after
murder, by Daisy Wells and Hazel Wong.

4

Ruling out Mr MacLean and Mamzelle in one fell swoop (both of them had seemed so promising!) was oddly disappointing, but what happened after lunch very nearly made up for it. First thing on Wednesday afternoon is Dance in the Gym, and *that* means an hour of torturously bobbing about in circles while Miss Hopkins watches us, her brown hair bouncing out of its clips, and says, 'Straight backs, girls! Straight arms, *straighten* those legs!' If we all turned into boards she would still not be perfectly satisfied with us.

She is particularly displeased with me. She pokes at my waistband and says, 'Perhaps a little more dancing might help with this, Hazel? Now, for heaven's sake *stand up straight.*'

Well, if I upset Miss Hopkins, Miss Hopkins certainly upsets me. I think she is horrible, and I do wish Daisy wasn't so obsessed with her.

That lesson, though, I almost had too much to think about to mind being in Dance. It was the first time I had been back in the Gym since *it* happened, and although it was tidy and ordinary, the floor polished to a shine by Jones the handyman, I still found myself shivering and twitching with nerves. When I walked through the doorway at the beginning of the lesson, I stumbled, and Daisy had to clap me on the back and whisper, 'Buck up, Hazel!' to get me moving again.

We began to dance. *One*-two-three, *one*-two-three, round in circles I moved, staring about me at the great big glassy windows and balance beams, and feeling amazed that nothing in the Gym had changed at all.

Round and round we danced, faster and faster, and then I looked over towards the balcony and caught sight of that little dark stain on the floorboards. Jones had obviously tried to scrub it away, but it was still there underneath the polish. Suddenly I remembered how Miss Bell had looked lying there, and how her head had rolled away from me in that awful, sloppy movement.

Forgetting Daisy's command to buck up, I turned my head in fascination and bumped into Beanie. Beanie squealed and grabbed at my gym tunic, I tripped against her and we both went crashing to the floor.

The fall was painful, but Miss Hopkins's response to it was extremely surprising. Instead of bawling at us, she merely came over to where we were lying (I flinched automatically) and said, 'Goodness, girls, how careless of you. Come on now, get up.' It was a miracle, I thought. Or – wait, was *this* suspicious behaviour? Was this the sort of thing those detectives in Daisy's books would make a note of? I peered up at Miss Hopkins, and decided that there was definitely something wrong with her. She was looking at me and *smiling*.

Still wondering what it could mean, I tried to get to my feet. Then I yelped and hurriedly sat back down again. My ankle was in agony.

'Oh dear,' said Miss Hopkins, still with that same bewilderingly cheerful look on her face. 'You've twisted it. It'll be quite all right in a while, but don't worry about finishing the lesson. Come along, Beanie, *you're* not hurt. Up you get. What is it, Daisy?'

Daisy, of course, had come running over as soon as she saw me fall down.

'Miss Hopkins, can I take Hazel to San?' she asked.

'Oh, yes, why not,' said Miss Hopkins. Now, I know that Miss Hopkins adores Daisy almost as much as Daisy adores her, but that sort of request from anyone ought to have made her suspicious. It didn't. What on earth had *happened* to Miss Hopkins? 'Thank you Daisy. All right, the rest of you, back to work!'

And just like that, Dance carried on without us. It was nearly the most surprising thing to happen all week – apart from finding Miss Bell's dead body, of course.

5

Daisy pulled me to my feet, and we hobbled three-legged out of the Gym.

'Daisy!' I gasped, partly from amazement and partly from the pain in my ankle, which was awfully bad. 'Something's up with Miss Hopkins! She's behaving extremely strangely! Did you see her just now? I think it might be suspicious behaviour.'

Daisy scowled at me. 'Hazel,' she said, 'you must *stop* accusing mistresses who we know can't be suspects.'

'I'm not accusing her! I only—'

'Miss Hopkins was up in the Pavilion Monday evening. She couldn't possibly have done it. All that's happened is that you've given us a lovely excuse to wander round the school and do some detective work.'

'Oh, all right,' I said, a bit cross that she was ignoring what I had said. 'But can I at least see Minny first for my ankle?' By Minny I meant Nurse Minn in the school sanatorium, our little sick-bay; girls go there with anything from a cut knee to pneumonia. You can pop by to get bandaged up or stay there for days if you're really ill. *San* sounds like a horrid doctor's office, but it is much nicer than that. Nurse Minn is lovely, with the kind of comfortable plumpness you want to bury your face in, and she gives out cups of tea and sweets even if your fever is only the made-up sort.

I thought that visiting Minny would have nothing to do with our investigation, but as it turned out, it gave us our next important lead.

When we got to San, there was already someone in Nurse Minn's consulting room. Daisy and I had to hover in the little hallway, waiting, and I realized that the person being looked after was King Henry herself. We could not help overhearing what she and Minny were saying – although Daisy did bump me closer and closer to the half-open door so as not to miss anything.

The first person we heard properly was King Henry. 'Oh, don't worry about me, it's perfectly – augh – all right.'

Minny tutted. 'Oh my love, your poor foot!' she said. 'Jones is dreadful for not getting it tidied up quicker.'

'Oh, he's been so terribly busy lately!' said King Henry. 'But he's working on it now. I only stepped on a stray piece of glass.'

'Hmm,' said Minny. '*What* did he say happened, again?'

'He thinks it was burglars,' said King Henry. 'It must have happened last night. They didn't steal anything, though.'

'Oh dear, don't look so worried!' cried Minny. 'I'm sure it wasn't, and even if it was, Miss Griffin will sort it all out in no time. New Wing corridor, was it? Yes, well, no harm done. None of us really *liked* those windows, did we?'

Daisy jabbed me in the ribs, and when I turned round, she was staring at me, eyes wide with excitement. 'Hazel!' she hissed. 'A clue!'

I did not see why a window broken on Tuesday night had anything to do with Miss Bell being murdered on Monday evening, but I learned a long time ago not to say anything when Daisy gets that look on her face.

'This could be important,' said Daisy. 'I must go hunt it down. Say hello to Minny for me!' And before I could say anything she had rushed away down the stairs in a fearful hurry. By the time King Henry came out into the corridor, limping on her newly-bandaged foot, I was all alone.

While I was having my ankle bound up by Nurse Minn – which was not a very nice experience – and eating a

biscuit – which was – Daisy was running through Deepdean looking for Jones.

Jones, as I have said before, is the Deepdean handyman. He lurks about in overalls, scowling at everyone
and threatening the shrimps, who he seems to think of
as a breed of larger and more troublesome mouse. He
has been here for as long as old Miss Lappet, and is
as much a part of Deepdean as Miss Griffin, though a
part that gets tidied away on open days and whenever
benefactors are about.

It was perhaps lucky that I was not with Daisy, since I
make Jones nervous. Whenever he speaks to me he uses
a very loud voice, as if I were slow, and looks at my left
ear. This is particularly odd, since he has one eye that
points right at all times. Daisy, on the other hand, is one
of Jones's favourites. I think he sees her the way I used
to, as the perfect English Miss, so he gives her slightly
pocket-squashed sweets and bashful smiles whenever
she passes him in the corridor.

Daisy found Jones exactly where she knew he would
be. Just where New Wing corridor turns into Music
Wing, there is a carved wooden archway with painted
glass panels set into it. The panels show the nine Muses,
in white nightdresses with drooping Pre-Raphaelite
hair, dripping bundles of flowers. They all look a bit
like Miss Tennyson. An artistic benefactor, who is also
an Old Girl, painted the Muses onto the glass herself,

which means we all have to be very polite about them and not mention that Clio, the Muse of History, has six toes and only one arm.

Or at least, she used to. Daisy arrived to find that several of the Muses were no more. Something had smashed into the lower panels, hard. Six-toed Clio was gone, and what had been a painting of Terpsichore being attacked by blue lilies was now just a jagged hole. Jones had started to hammer bits of board over the archway.

'Hallo, Jones!' said Daisy.

'Hello, Miss Daisy,' said Jones. 'Not in lessons, then?'

'I came to see *you*, Jones,' said Daisy in her most friendly voice. 'I heard there was a burglary and I wanted to help.'

Jones frowned. 'Ah, but I don't think it *was* burglars now,' he said. 'Nothing's missing, you see. There's just chaos everywhere. And poor Miss Henrietta's hurt her foot! I blame those shrimps.' And he launched into a long complaint about the state of the school during the past few days. 'But when I spoke to Miss Griffin about it, she told me not to worry! Not worry, I ask you! The only consolation is this – come and look!' He beckoned Daisy over to one of the panels. 'See this?' he asked her. 'This says to me that whatever vandal did it is already getting their comeuppance.'

He pointed, and Daisy bent in to see. There, on a bit of blue glass, was a long rusty stain.

'Blood!' said Jones triumphantly. 'They cut themselves good and proper. Well, I hope it hurt, because I shall be cleaning up their mess all day at this rate.'

It was at this point that Miss Griffin came striding down New Wing stairs, her neat pale legs encased as usual in her silk stockings and grey tweed skirt. She was coming from her office, which is on the upper floor of the wing, and she looked very annoyed when she saw Daisy standing there.

'Daisy Wells!' she said, pausing majestically halfway down. 'Whatever are you doing out of lessons?'

'Taking a message to Mr Reid,' said Daisy promptly. 'From Miss Lappet. She wants to know if he could take her second-form class next lesson, because she has to cover Science now that, you know, Miss Bell has gone.'

Miss Griffin was not impressed. 'Well, you had better not waste any more time talking to Jones, had you?' she snapped.

'Yes, Miss Griffin,' said Daisy, then, 'No, Miss Griffin. Sorry, Miss Griffin!'

'Run along then,' said Miss Griffin, waving her hand like the Queen. Daisy ran along.

If there is one thing that makes Daisy such a good liar, it is that when she lies, she lies *thoroughly*. By the time she came back to where I was waiting for her in San – with my left ankle well wrapped up and two extra biscuits from Nurse Minn in my pocket – The One had agreed to Miss Lappet's phantom request, and five minutes after I hobbled into our History lesson Daisy had Miss Lappet convinced that she had actually asked Daisy to take the message in the first place. 'You are a treasure, Daisy,' said Miss Lappet, folding her arms over her massive bosom (her cardigan had been buttoned up wrong that day, and it made her look even more misshapen than usual) and blinking down at Daisy through her little glasses. 'Whatever would the school do without you?'

'I don't know, Miss,' said Daisy primly. 'I'm sure everyone would manage *somehow*.'

6

'I don't understand,' I said to Daisy, on our way up to House at the end of the day (slowly, because of my ankle), 'what Jones's broken window has to do with the murder.'

'Well,' said Daisy, stepping aside to let Lavinia rush past after a second-form shrimp, – 'first of all, it's out of the ordinary. And isn't the first rule of detection to consider everything out of the ordinary as potentially important?'

I thought of Miss Hopkins, but I knew that even if I reminded Daisy of her odd behaviour, it still wouldn't count.

'And secondly, there's what *hasn't* happened. No one apart from King Henry has gone to Minny's with a cut that could have been caused by that glass.'

'How do you know?' I objected.

'Hazel,' said Daisy, 'have you *ever* known Nurse Minn to hear about something and not tell the story ten times over? If someone had come in earlier, with exactly the same sort of cut, King Henry's injury would have reminded her of it. If she didn't tell you about the amazing coincidence—'

'Which she didn't,' I admitted, thinking this was exactly why Daisy was the President of the Detective Society, and I was only the Secretary.

'—then it certainly didn't happen. Which means that whoever cut themselves hasn't reported it, and *that* means they were too afraid to. And we know it must be someone from school – if it had been robbers, Jones would have found other signs of a break-in from outside, and told us about it. What I think is this: last night the murderer came back to move Miss Bell's body out of the school from wherever it had been hidden since Monday evening. They used the Cupboard trolley again, crashed it into the archway, smashed the glass and cut themselves.'

'But,' I said, 'why wasn't Miss Bell moved on Monday evening?'

'The murderer had to decide what to do with the body. Perhaps they planned to keep it in school, and then realized they couldn't?'

'But nobody found it yesterday!' I said. 'It can't have been that bad a hiding place.'

'Indeed,' said Daisy. 'Actually, I've been thinking about that. It ought to be the next part of our mission: the Hunt for the Hiding Place of Miss Bell's Body. That sounds just like a treasure hunt, doesn't it? Like hunt the slipper, but with a body.'

'Oh, *no*,' I said. I knew perfectly well that looking for a body would be nothing like hunting for a slipper. 'Daisy, I—'

At this point we were interrupted by Beanie scurrying up to us. 'Hello,' she said eagerly, skipping along beside Daisy. 'What's up?'

'Er,' I said. 'We were—'

'We were just discussing Miss Bell,' Daisy finished smoothly.

'Ooh!' said Beanie, wrapping her red and blue House scarf round her hands and nearly dropping her school bag. 'Exciting. D'you think she's been kidnapped by the East— Oh sorry, Hazel.'

Beanie is one of the only people at Deepdean who would have thought to apologize for that.

'I heard she'd resigned,' I said, to thank her.

'No!' said Beanie, who in her own kind-hearted way was as much of a gossip as Kitty. 'But Miss Griffin was going to announce her as the new Deputy! Unless she was too upset by The One jilting her to care . . .'

'Hmm,' I said. 'Perhaps.'

'Oh, I do hate it when people quarrel,' said Beanie

unhappily. 'I almost wish she *had* been kidnapped by a gang – or would that be worse?'

'*Much* worse,' said Daisy, hitching her bag up onto her shoulder and elbowing Beanie to cheer her up. Beanie is so like a little dog that not even Daisy, who doesn't usually bother much about other people's feelings, can bear seeing her disappointed. 'I heard they go about stabbing knives into gang members who are disloyal, and then they leave horrible messages for the family in their loved one's blood.'

Beanie's good-natured brown eyes widened in fascinated horror.

'Stabbing and that sort of thing is absolutely rife in Russia, my uncle says,' Daisy continued.

'Wells!' said Virginia Overton, who was walking past and heard Daisy. 'That's a fearful lie! Don't you believe her, Martineau.'

'I didn't,' said Beanie quickly. 'I'm perfectly all right.'

Virginia sniffed. 'I hope so,' she said. 'I've got my eye on you, Wells.'

We finished the walk up to House talking about Beanie's pony, Boggles, whom she had left at home and missed passionately. Daisy, in turn, began to tell a story about her pony, Gladstone, who was a genius and had once jumped a six-foot hedge. They chattered away, and I stared up through the empty tree branches at the tall houses and the darkening sky, and worried and worried about the murder.

Was it really the murderer who had smashed those windows? And if so, was it while they were removing Miss Bell's body from the school? Where had it been hidden in the meantime? . . . And, most importantly of all, who was the murderer? We had established alibis for Mamzelle, Mr MacLean, and Miss Hopkins, but Miss Lappet, Miss Parker, Miss Tennyson and The One still had no alibis at all, and they had all been near the Gym at the right time. Which of them had done it?

PART FOUR

WE HAVE OUR SUSPICIONS, AND AN ARGUMENT

1

In Prayers on Thursday morning, after a stern notice about the value of the windows in New Wing corridor and the importance of owning up to mistakes, as an honourable Deepdean girl ought, Miss Griffin finally broke the news that we had all been waiting for.

'As you may have noticed,' she said from the lectern, 'Miss Bell has not been in attendance this week. Unfortunately, I must now inform you that she has resigned her post. Until a suitable replacement can be found, the other masters and mistresses will be taking your Science lessons. I ask you all to be mindful of the additional work that they will be doing, and I hope that this will put an end to the rather irresponsible gossip that I have been hearing lately regarding Miss Bell's absence.' She stared severely down at us over her little gold-rimmed reading glasses, and several girls looked away. For a moment even I felt rather guilty.

Then everyone woke up to what she had said, and up and down the rows, girls began nudging one another in excitement. The 'irresponsible gossip' had not been stopped at all. King Henry looked around, her face pale with fury. I wondered if her foot was still hurting. Her glare made the nudging die down for a bit, but it started up again as soon as she looked away.

'Are you sure we ought to still be investigating?' I asked Daisy as we filed out of Prayers.

'Don't be stupid, Hazel!' she hissed back at me. 'You *know* the Bell hasn't really resigned. She's still just as dead as she ever was, and we're the only ones who know the truth. Think of her family, Hazel. If we don't find out what really happened, no one ever will.'

It was awful of Daisy, bringing up Miss Bell's family like that – and just like her too. She knew it would make me worry, and of course it did. I imagined Miss Bell's mother. She was probably widowed, living alone in a single cold room, just as poor as Miss Bell had been.

This was very upsetting. I much preferred assuming that mistresses had no lives at all; that if I went into Deepdean during the hols I would find them all wandering about in the corridors, giving lessons in empty rooms. But once I had imagined Miss Bell's tragic mother, I could not make her vanish.

And of course, Daisy knew it.

As we marched along the marble chessboard of

Library corridor in our neat grey two-by-two rows, both Daisy and I were quiet. I was thinking about Miss Bell's mother and getting more and more upset. Daisy was probably thinking about the murder, and fashionable hats, and who cheated in the Maths test, all at once, as though she is really three people instead of one.

Two rows behind us, Kitty whispered something to Beanie just as we passed Miss Parker, who was on duty outside the mistresses' common room, and who began bellowing at them as though they had been caught spitting on the Bible.

Our row faltered to a stop, and the girls directly behind us began to bunch up and crane over each other in excitement as Miss Parker tore her hands through her hair and howled in red-faced fury. Of course, we are all used to Miss Parker's rages, but this was something quite different. Bawling about disgraces to the school, she gave Kitty and Beanie detention twice and then forgot what she had already said and gave them another one for good measure.

We all stayed very quiet and still so as not to attract her attention, the way you would with a tiger in the zoo. But all the same she caught Lavinia goggling at her and howled: 'ALL of you others, MOVE OFF! Hurry up or I'll have the lot of you, I'll—'

At this point, though, Miss Griffin came through the packed corridor and put a calming hand on Miss

Parker's shoulder. Miss Griffin has an eerie way of knowing where she is needed, and being there.

Miss Parker gasped at the touch, and all the fight went out of her. Even her hair sagged.

'Come along, Miss Parker,' said Miss Griffin cheerfully, as though they were both at a garden party and late for the tea. 'Move along, girls, otherwise you'll be late for your lessons.' And that was that. If Miss Griffin tells you to do something, you had better do it. Everyone drifted away, quickly but reluctantly, and the corridor was soon back to normal again. But Daisy, walking in very proper silence next to me, turned her head and widened her eyes at me in a way that I knew meant, *Suspicious behaviour from Parker again.*

2

Miss Parker was not the only one of our prime suspects to be behaving suspiciously. Our second lesson on Thursdays is English with Miss Tennyson, who wanted the Deputy job but was beaten to it by Miss Bell. Miss Tennyson, as I have said, is a fearful drip, and terribly nervous. Her large soppy eyes well up like a squeezed sponge at everything from poetry to animals, and because we are doing the great poets this term, we had to endure a weeping fit from Miss Tennyson nearly every lesson.

That day, she had Daisy read out Gray's 'Elegy in a Country Churchyard'. From the shape her mouth made, I knew Daisy found it utter tosh, but she read it well, as she always does, in a clear, calm voice that did not betray what she was thinking.

But as she read I noticed – as did Daisy, though she did not show it – that Miss Tennyson was being more than usually weepy.

'*Each in his narrow cell for ever laid,*' read Daisy in appropriately funereal tones. Miss Tennyson turned pale. In fact, every reference to graves or dead people (there are lots in Gray's 'Elegy', in case you have not been forced to read it yet yourself) had Miss Tennyson twitching like a science experiment. When Daisy reached the lines,

> *Can storied urn or animated bust*
> *Back to its mansion call the fleeting breath?*

Miss Tennyson began shaking so hard I thought she might fall off her chair, and after the last line she sat in silence for so long that we all started looking at each other in real concern.

'Are you all right, Miss Tennyson?' asked Beanie nervously at last.

'Perfectly, Beanie dear,' said Miss Tennyson, dabbing at her cheeks with her handkerchief. 'I thought Daisy's reading was *so* lovely that I wanted to give us all time to contemplate it.'

I could tell it was an excuse, and a weak one. Not even Miss Tennyson cared about poetry *that* much.

That was when Daisy pounced. 'Miss Tennyson,' she said, putting up her hand, 'may I ask you something?'

'Is it about Gray's "Elegy?"' asked Miss Tennyson.

'No,' said Daisy. 'It's about Miss Bell.'

Miss Tennyson dropped the book of poems she was

holding. It clattered onto the desk and the third form all stared from her to Daisy and back again.

'I need to ask Miss Bell something, but now she's resigned I don't know where to write to her. I don't suppose *you* know where she's gone to, do you?'

'Why would you think that *I* would have any idea where Miss Bell has gone?' asked Miss Tennyson, so quietly it was almost a whisper. She had turned as pale as one of Gray's poetical gravestones.

'Oh, *I* don't know,' Daisy said breezily. 'I thought she might have said where she was going. It was only a hope.'

Miss Tennyson turned red, a specklish flush that broke out all down her neck and into her high-collared blouse. 'Daisy Wells!' she said. 'This has nothing to do with poetry. I'll thank you to keep on topic for the rest of the lesson. Otherwise – otherwise you will be doing extra composition for me in Detention.'

We all gaped at her. We had never heard Miss Tennyson make that kind of threat before. Even last term when Lavinia said *King Lear* was idiotic, Miss Tennyson had only sighed and looked wounded. This threat was quite out of character, and it had come because Daisy had mentioned Miss Bell.

Miss Tennyson did not want to talk about Miss Bell, and a poem about graves was making her upset. She had just moved to the very top of our suspect list.

3

In the afternoon we had Games, which meant I had to stand shivering on the playing field while Daisy and the rest of the sporty girls galloped around and screamed at each other. That day my ankle gave me an excuse to be in defence (although I was not allowed to skip Games altogether – that would not be the Deepdean way), so at least I could shiver in peace while the ball was hammered to and fro in front of me.

Unfortunately, being in defence meant being next to Lavinia. If it is possible, she is even worse at Games than I am, which makes her terribly sulky. Miss Hopkins has given up on her entirely, so Lavinia just lumps about near goal, glaring at everyone.

It was a very English afternoon. The air was full of water droplets that clung to our faces and weighed down our clothes, and the grass had turned into a particularly slimy sort of mud. I wrapped my arms round myself and shivered. It was the sort of weather that Daisy loves. She rocketed about the pitch, skirt flapping, and winged the ball at goal so hard that we had to dive out of the way to save ourselves. Miss Hopkins cheered and waved her hockey stick in encouragement. She was still in an astonishingly happy mood.

I was trying to observe her when Lavinia began to speak to me. 'Daisy's *annoyingly* brilliant, isn't she?' she said as she watched Daisy tackle Clementine.

'Daisy's not annoying!' I said. 'She's just *Daisy*.'

'Well, you would say that,' said Lavinia. 'You're practically her slave.'

'I am not!' I said furiously. 'Daisy's my best friend.'

'Huh,' said Lavinia. 'Some friend. She uses you – haven't you noticed? And she only took an interest in you because you're an Oriental. Her uncle is a spy – that's why foreigners interest her.'

Now, if it is bad form to show your emotions in England, it is even more so in Hong Kong, so I know I should feel most terribly guilty about what happened next. Unfortunately, I do not feel guilty at all.

The ball was coming down the field again, with Daisy pounding along after it while Kitty whacked at her stick and tried to trip her up. I watched the ball jump and roll over tufts of muddy grass towards us. Lavinia had not noticed it. Daisy gave the ball one more whack and it arced up in the air and landed just next to Lavinia's right foot.

That was enough for me. I launched myself at Lavinia, whirling my hockey stick, and crashed into her as hard as I could. For the second time in a week, I fell down in a tangle of legs and arms and games knickers. 'Oh!' I shrieked, sounding as horrified as I could manage.

Then I scrambled up, making sure that my stick dug into Lavinia's middle and my knee squashed into her thigh. My shoe scratched down her leg, leaving it streaky with mud. Lavinia kicked back, hard, on my ankle, and I toppled over again.

'Beast!' panted Lavinia, and scratched me.

The game had stopped, and Miss Hopkins was running over to us. It turned out that her cheerfulness only stretched so far. 'HAZEL, NOT AGAIN!' she bellowed.

'I was trying to get the ball,' I said. 'I tripped.'

Lavinia dragged herself to her feet and pulled me up with her. 'We both tripped,' she said, breathing hard. 'It wasn't Hazel's fault.' That's the good thing about Lavinia. She can be foully mean, and she's vicious in a fight, but at least she doesn't hold grudges afterwards.

'I can see perfectly well that that's a lie,' said Miss Hopkins, sighing. 'Hazel, in this country we do not fight. We are *civilized*. This is the second time you have knocked over a classmate this week. Go and get changed back into your school things, and if I ever catch you doing something like this again I shall send you to Miss Griffin. Lavinia, play on. Hazel, *go*!'

It was not really a punishment, or at least not one as bad as Miss Hopkins would usually have given out, but it still stung. Cheeks burning, I turned and marched off towards the pavilion. I felt swollen up with anger. I couldn't see why Lavinia wasn't being punished as well. She had fought back, after all. And she had been so horrid about Daisy! It was not true that Daisy was only friends with me because I was from Hong Kong. She was not like that at all, I told myself. But all the same, there was a bit of me that was worried. Could it really be true?

I changed back into my school things, my heart rocketing about inside my chest like a dynamo. My ankle was aching again, but I ignored it. I had hardly finished pulling my socks on, though, when the door of the changing-room banged open. I crouched down, thinking that it might be Miss Hopkins. But the person who stuck their head through a row of pinafores and grinned at me was not Miss Hopkins at all, but Daisy.

Her golden hair was stiff with mud and there was mud on one of her cheeks too. As she burrowed through the clothes and wiggled her way out onto the bench opposite me, she left quite a lot of mud behind her, but she didn't seem to mind.

'Wotcher, Watson!' said Daisy. 'I've come to join you, even though you *were* rude to Miss Hopkins. I thought this would be a good opportunity to hold a Detective Society meeting.'

There was Daisy, adoring Miss Hopkins again. I decided to ignore it. 'What did you do to get out of Games?' I asked.

'I told Hopkins I had the curse and she let me go.' Daisy said this without a blush, as though it was the easiest thing in the world. Perhaps it was; for her.

'Daisy,' I said. 'Do you know what Lavinia said to me?'

'No,' said Daisy. 'What awful lies has she been telling this time?'

'She said . . . that you were only friends with me because I come from Hong Kong.'

There was a pause. 'What utter tosh,' said Daisy. 'As you know perfectly well, I'm only friends with you because you were so persistent about it that I couldn't refuse.'

'*Daisy!*' I said.

'All right. That's nonsense. I'm friends with you because you are the cleverest person in this whole school.'

I blushed. It was one of the nicest things she had ever said to me.

'Apart, of course, from me.'

Daisy couldn't bear not having the last word. 'Well, now that we've cleared that up, can we get on to the real business? We won't have another opportunity like this all day. Ready, Watson?'

'Ready,' I said, pulling my casebook out of my bag and trying to put my mind to Detective Society business.

'Excellent,' said Daisy. 'Now, we've already made some really important discoveries, but before we go any further we need to talk about suspects. We're agreed that we've narrowed our suspect list down to four: Miss Parker, Miss Tennyson, Miss Lappet and The One. The others all have good alibis – and although in books they might have done it by constructing a dastardly long-range missile out of a trombone, three plant pots and the Gym vaulting horse, in real life that sort of thing does seem beyond the bounds of possibility.'

I nodded. Daisy was right.

'So, the top of our list is Miss Tennyson,' I said. 'She wanted the Deputy job. She was down at school for Lit. Soc, but that finished at five twenty. We saw her by the Gym half an hour later, but we have no idea where she was in between those times. And what about today's English lesson!'

'Wasn't that a sight?' agreed Daisy. 'She certainly *behaved* guiltily.'

'And then there's Miss Parker. We know that she lied about her alibi. She was at school when Kitty saw her just after socs finished, and so she had the perfect opportunity to commit the murder. She has a motive too – jealousy about Miss Bell and The One – and she has been raging about the school all week. That could be her guilty conscience. So that's two who seem promising, and don't appear to have alibis. What about the others? Let's see – The One, and Miss Lappet.

'The One first. We know he stayed down after school to teach Sophie Croke-Finchley piano that evening, but the lesson ended at four fifty. After that, he was free, and we saw that he was in his cubby at five fifty – again, near the Gym at the correct time. We shall just have to watch him.'

'Miss Lappet,' I said, looking up from my casebook. 'Like Miss Tennyson, she wanted the Deputy job. She went to Miss Griffin's office at four thirty, but we don't have an alibi for her after that. Although – do we know when she came out again? If she stayed there until after the time of the murder, that'd give her an excellent alibi. She'd have had Miss Griffin watching over her all evening.'

'Oh, good work, Watson,' said Daisy. 'We should look into it at the first opportunity. You know, I'd say we were doing rather well. Down to four suspects already! Our next plan of action should be more of the same – we keep hunting down alibis, or lack of them, and we watch our four like hawks while we're at it. *Constant vigilance.* Oh, and about that other thing – I've come up with a really excellent idea that will give us time to hunt round for where the murderer hid Miss Bell's body, in between killing her on Monday and moving it out of the school on Tuesday.'

She said it so casually that I thought she must be joking. 'Don't be silly,' I said. 'You can't have done. There's always someone around the school watching us, no matter what time of day it is.'

'Exactly,' said Daisy. 'That's why my idea's such a corker. I can't tell you what it is yet, though, in case it goes wrong.'

'Daisy! Why not?'

'Don't argue, Watson! Aren't I the President of the Detective Society? That means that I'm allowed to have a plan without telling you.'

I opened my mouth to say that I couldn't see why, but then shut it again crossly. I knew there was no point. Arguing with Daisy about things like that is like arguing with an avalanche when it is already on its way down the mountain. It was no good wanting to know anything about Daisy's mysterious plan. She would tell me when she wanted to, or not at all.

I was still trying not to be furious about it when the changing-room door banged open again and Kitty, Beanie and the rest of the form rushed in. Daisy began loudly talking about Amy Johnson's daring flight to Cape Town, so I took a calming breath and joined in.

4

Considering Lavinia, and what she said, it's funny to remember what I used to think of Daisy. Last year, when I first came to Deepdean, she was exactly in the middle of our form, neither a swot nor a dunce. Her English essays were utterly dull, her French hopped tenses like anything, and she mixed up the Habsburgs and the Huns. The mistresses were fond of her, but – 'Daisy dear,' said Miss Lappet one day, peering down through her little glasses, 'you are a charming girl, but you are certainly not cut out for an academic life.'

'I don't mind,' said Daisy in reply. 'I don't want to be a Bluestocking. I shall marry a Lord.' The whole second form squealed with laughter and Miss Lappet folded her arms over her cushiony bosom but looked amused. In fact, as we all knew, Daisy had no need to marry a Lord. Her father already was one, a real one with ermine robes and a country seat in Gloucestershire.

It was this sort of thing that made Daisy so fascinating. Almost all the younger shrimps had pashes on her. (A *pash*, in case you haven't heard the word before, is school talk for something that is rather difficult to describe – I suppose it's being in love, but different somehow, and so quite all right with everyone.) I was as much taken with the Honourable Daisy Wells as anyone else, and so things might have gone on if it were not for something that happened halfway through my first term at Deepdean.

It was late on a Thursday afternoon, and Miss Lappet was struggling to give us a lesson about Charles I. 'Don't be so slow,' she snapped at Beanie, who had just given her third wrong answer in a row. 'Great heavens, I might as well be speaking Hottentot. Before I go quite mad – and I *shall*, mark my words – I don't suppose by some miracle Daisy will prove to know when – Lord grant me patience – the Long Parliament was first called?'

Daisy was idly drawing something in her exercise book. Caught off guard, she looked up. 'Third of November 1640,' she said without even pausing to think.

Miss Lappet gaped at her. 'Why – Daisy!' she gasped, amazed, sitting down in her chair with a heavy plump. 'That's the very day! However did you remember that?'

I happened to be looking at Daisy at the time, and for the merest of seconds something rather like panic flashed across her face. Then she blinked and the look disappeared, replaced by vague wide-eyed surprise. 'Oh! Did I really?' she asked breathlessly. 'What luck! Fancy that, Miss Lappet. I must be learning something after all.'

'Wonders shall never cease,' said Miss Lappet. 'Now if you could only recreate that in your essays they might become almost respectable.'

Daisy blinked up at Miss Lappet. 'I'm afraid that's *quite* out of the question, Miss,' she said in tones of deep despair.

'Of course it is,' sighed Miss Lappet as the rest of the second form giggled supportively.

The lesson continued, but I was thinking about Daisy's answer. She had known it so very quickly – quicker than even I could manage. If it had been anyone else, I would have thought them a swot – but Daisy Wells did not swot. Everyone knew that.

Nevertheless, I could not help suspecting that she had known the answer. It had not just been a lucky guess. Over the next few weeks I watched Daisy closely in all our lessons, and as I did so I became convinced that, far from being someone who struggled just enough for the mistresses to be encouraging and the other girls to think her a card, Daisy knew everything she was ever asked.

She wanted to seem a fool, and she was pausing or flubbing her responses because she had decided that a particular fact was not something she ought to remember. The Daisy Wells we all pashed on was, in short, not real at all, but a very clever part. I watched her running about, shrieking, turning cartwheels and looking as though she did not care about anything apart from beating St Simmonds at lacrosse on Saturday, and I began to see that all the time there was a different Daisy underneath. A Daisy who not only knew the name of every one of the men who had helped Guy Fawkes in his plot but the reason why Belinda Vance in the fifth form was staying so late at school, and what Elsie Drew-Peters said to Heather Montefiore to make her cry. She was always gathering up information on people – not to blackmail them or do anything awful like that, that's not Daisy at all – but just to know things.

Daisy always has to *know* things.

5

As soon as we got back up to House after Games that afternoon, Daisy began to work on her top-secret plan. Thursday afternoon tea, which is served in the House Dining Room to all girls not at Socs that day, is cream buns. I had two, which was blissful, but I could not help noticing that Daisy spent most of her tea not eating at all. She was deep in conversation with the fifth former Alice Murgatroyd. This was odd. There were lots of rumours going round about Alice – that she has a secret cigarette stash in her tuck box, for example – and it is simply not usual for girls from different forms to spend afternoon tea together. But just as other people began to wonder at what was going on, Daisy and Alice nodded to each other and Daisy came back to sit down at the third-form table. She nudged Kitty, and whispered something, and Kitty whispered to Beanie.

'Psst!' hissed Beanie, leaning over to me. 'Midnight feast tonight! Daisy says so.'

I nudged Lavinia, and passed the message on, but inside I was surprised. Surely Daisy was too busy with her plan to bother about things like midnight feasts. There is an awful lot to decide on for a midnight feast – what prank to play on which other dorm, what cakes to ask everyone to bring, and when to set the alarm clock under your pillow for. Then there is the matter of secrecy. At Deepdean I have learned that it is very important, when you are having a midnight feast, not to let anything slip about it. Otherwise the other dorms know that a prank is coming and prepare themselves – or, worse, plan a counter-prank. But that afternoon Daisy fired off order after whispered order, and soon all five of us knew exactly what we had to do.

The whole of our dorm kept exemplary silence about the upcoming feast, although at toothbrushes Beanie got quite giggly when the prefect on duty (it was King Henry that evening) told us to go to bed. Daisy had to wink sternly to quieten her down, and we were lucky that King Henry was too preoccupied to notice. Then we all lay down in our beds demurely, and King Henry clicked off the light and closed the door. The block of yellow light falling onto Lavinia's bed vanished, and the dorm went dark.

I must have fallen asleep at once.

I was woken by people shuffling about. There was a *thump* and a giggle from Beanie, then Lavinia hissed, 'Beans! Don't knock into me like that, you idiot!'

'Sorry, Lavinia,' whispered Beanie, and tripped over something else.

I sat up. Someone had pulled back the curtain at the far end of the dorm, and in the moonlight (rather dim, as the moon was mostly behind the clouds) I could see several people huddled round Daisy's bed. Beanie must have fallen over Lavinia on the way there; they were now crouched on the floor picking up their cakes.

I climbed out of bed, put on my slippers and pulled open my tuck box. The week before I had received two parcels. One was a green and gold Fortnum and Mason's gift box with a note that said, *From your father. Don't tell your mother.* The other was wrapped in brown paper, smothered with stamps, and had come with a note in our chauffeur's painstaking print: *Your esteemed mother sends you this gift. She wishes you to not inform your esteemed father.* My mother always makes the servants write for her – I don't know why, she can write perfectly well herself since my father taught her.

The brown paper parcel was full of lotus-paste

moon cakes from our kitchen. They are my favourite food, sweet and heavy on my tongue, like nothing here in England; but all the same I wish my mother would not send them. Lavinia saw one once, and for weeks after told everyone that I ate heathen pies. Luckily, the Fortnum's box had proper English walnut cake in it, and not even Lavinia could sniff at that. I took it out, stuffed the moon cakes back into my tuck box, under a pile of Angela Brazil books, and went to join the feast.

'Welcome,' whispered Daisy, waving her torch in my face. 'What have you got?'

'Walnut cake,' I whispered back.

'Excellent,' said Daisy. 'Add it to the rest of the pile. Once Beanie and Lavinia get over here – come *on*, Beanie – we can begin.'

'Sorry,' whispered Beanie, hurrying over. 'I've got chocolate cake and tongue, if that helps.'

'It does,' said Daisy grandly. 'Now let's eat – I'm starving.'

For a while, everyone ate in silence.

'Pass the tongue,' said Daisy, with her mouth full.

(Privately, I cannot understand the way English people eat their meat – in dull sauceless lumps which all taste exactly the same – but I have learned to swallow it down as quickly as possible and say 'Delicious!' at the end of it.)

Lavinia passed over the tin. 'Tongue is nice with chocolate cake,' she said as she did so. 'You wouldn't think it would be, but it is. You should try it.'

'I like it on biscuits,' said Kitty, munching. 'Daisy, what are we doing for a prank?'

'Ah,' said Daisy, 'well. That's been taken care of already. At this very moment there's a nice cold bucket of water balanced above the washroom door. It'll give the other third-form dorm a nice surprise tomorrow morning when they go for their showers!'

We all giggled appreciatively. The other dorm had taken to leaping up as soon as the wake-up bell rang and hogging the showers just so they could be down at breakfast first and get dorm points from Matron for promptness. It was odious of them and we had all been dying to get them back for it.

'We ought to do something else, though,' said Kitty. 'Right now. Otherwise it's not a proper midnight feast.'

'If only it was last year,' said Daisy offhandedly. 'Remember all those creepy things we used to do? Of course they were quite silly really, and we couldn't do them *now*, but—'

'Oh, but why not?' cried Kitty. 'We could try levitating Beanie again – remember when we did that?'

'Oh no,' wailed Beanie. 'Why is it always me who's the one being levitated? I hate it—'

'Because you're the littlest, Beans,' said Lavinia. 'And besides, it's such fun when you squeal.'

'Well, I won't do it,' said Beanie, trying to be firm. 'I won't. You can't make me.'

'You know,' said Kitty, 'I've still got that old Ouija board in the bottom of my tuck box. We could have a go with that, if you like.'

'Oh no,' gasped Beanie, 'not a séance, please. It gives me the creeps.'

'Then you oughtn't to have said no to the levitating, Beanie,' said Lavinia. 'Kitty, get out the board.'

'Oh please,' wailed Beanie. 'Please no!'

'Shh!' said Kitty. 'You'll wake Matron!'

They both quietened down at once. Nobody wanted to have the midnight feast ruined by an angry Matron.

Daisy, I noticed, had taken no part in this. She was sitting back on her heels watching the argument. As I knew perfectly well, this meant that she was Up To Something.

Kitty went rooting through her tuck box, and after a minute or so gave a satisfied cry. Her Ouija board is from our Spiritualist Society days. It is just a bit of red cardboard, really, with black curly letters and numbers painted on it; and a yellow eye in the very middle of the board where the sharp triangular counter rests at the beginning. I always hated that eye, which glares up from the board as though it is watching you. To be truthful, I feel quite the same as Beanie about séances, although I never let on to Daisy about it.

Anyway, Daisy balanced her torch on her knees, so that its light fell onto the board, and we all rested our fingers on the counter, as you are supposed to. For a while, nothing happened. I listened to us all breathing, and stared and stared at the counter until the painted eye beneath it seemed to glow up at me.

Then, all at once, the counter moved. Kitty gave a little squeal, and quite a few of us jumped, so the counter jiggled about and the torchlight jolted.

'I don't like it,' Beanie whispered as we all watched the counter begin to slide upwards. 'I don't like it, I don't like it, I don't—'

'Shut it, Beanie,' hissed Lavinia fiercely, and Beanie was silent. The counter gave a little jump and came to rest over the letter H.

'H!' said Daisy. 'Something at last! Quick, Hazel, write it down!'

I sat back and snatched up my casebook, very glad to look away from that eye.

H, I wrote.

Meanwhile, the counter had moved left, to E, and was now on its way right again. I barely needed to wait for it to stop – L, of course. But then, just as I was about to automatically put down a second L, the counter gave a jerk and went surging off to the left to land, clear as anything, on the P.

Beanie let out a little squeak, and Kitty shushed her. My mouth felt very dry. But the board was not finished yet. Right it went, all the way, to M, U, R, and then back again to D, E, and finally came to rest on the R.

HELP. MURDER.

We looked around at each other. We were all pale, even Daisy – although, as I know well, it is never any good trying to work out what Daisy is really thinking.

It was Kitty who finally spoke.

'Who is this?' she whispered. 'Who are you?'

The counter wobbled. Then off it went again, slower this time: *M-I-S-S-B-E-L*—

I had a single moment of utter horror – and then, of course, I realized what was going on: Daisy must be moving the counter. I felt strangely cheated – just as I did when my father took me to the circus in Kowloon and I realized that their mermaid was only a sad little hairless monkey with a fish tail attached. As much as I didn't want the shade of Miss Bell to come back and haunt me, I was annoyed when I realized that our ghost was in fact just Daisy. So *this* was her secret plan! I wished, once again, that she would tell me things beforehand.

The counter was still moving.

'Miss Bell!' said Kitty, who always liked to be the one

to communicate with the other side. 'But you resigned – you're not dead.'

YES. DEAD.

Beanie squeaked.

'Shush, Beanie! You'll have Matron up here! How—'

NO TIME. HELP. MURDER.

'You were murdered?'

MURDER.

'By who?'

WHOM.

'I think she means, *by whom*,' said Daisy. She must have thought she was being very funny.

'It really *is* Miss Bell!' whispered Beanie. 'Oh . . .'

Then she fainted, very quietly, onto Kitty's shoulder.

NO TIME. MURDERER UNKNOWN. CANNOT REST.

'But what can we do?' asked Kitty.

TELL ALL. GUILT WILL OUT. HELP – Q – T – B – N – 2 –

After that the counter slid off the bottom of the board and no one could get any more sense out of it. Beanie had come out of her faint and was crying quietly.

'You're all babies. I wasn't afraid at all,' said Lavinia, and then she climbed into her bed, pulled her blanket all the way up over her head and refused to say anything more.

The midnight feast seemed to be over and I crept

back to my own bed. Beanie refused to sleep alone and had to be let into Kitty's bed for comfort. We could hear them whispering quietly to each other under the bedclothes.

I had closed my eyes and was trying to go back to sleep when there was a sudden creak, the side of my mattress dipped and someone slid under the covers next to me. In spite of myself, I gasped.

'Wotcher,' hissed Daisy in my ear.

'Ow!' I whispered, wriggling over. 'You're lying on my arm.'

'Never mind that,' Daisy whispered back, as quietly as she could. 'What did you think? Wasn't I good?'

'I think you were awful. Whatever did you do it for?'

'Don't you see? It was the only way. It doesn't matter what Miss Griffin said about Miss Bell having resigned; by tomorrow the news about her murder will be all over the school. The murderer will simply be hopping with panic – they're bound to do something that'll lead us straight to them. And anyone who knows anything, or saw anything, or knows of an alibi for any of our suspects will come forward. All we need to do is watch. And the best bit is, *I* won't look like I had anything to do with it at all. If you must know, I feel really rather clever.'

6

I didn't like the idea of the murderer panicking at all. What if they came after me because of it? I had another awful, sleepless night, and got up on Friday morning feeling sick to my stomach about the day to come.

Moments after the wake-up bell rang, while we were all sitting up in bed, we heard squeals ringing out from the washroom. It was the other third-form dorm, of course, running straight into our cold-water trap. Which reminded everyone of what had happened at the séance. We had hardly sat down to breakfast before Kitty had told five different people the story of Miss Bell's ghostly appearance. It went round the room like wildfire, and Daisy, listening to its progress, puffed up with pride. I wanted to shake her. She was putting us both in danger – but of course, she could not see it. She only thought she was being clever, and helping to solve the murder. I was almost glad when something happened to spoil her good mood.

'Ready for the match against St Chator's this weekend?' Daisy asked Clementine as she chewed a slice of toast. I think it was Daisy's way of making peace for the bucket of water. 'I heard Hopkins was awfully helpful at the tactics session in the Pavilion on Monday evening.'

Clementine sniffed. 'If we *are* ready, it's no thanks to Hopkins,' she said. 'The session wasn't even halfway through when she dodged down to school with some silly excuse about needing to write a letter. A letter! When we haven't beaten Chator's for four years! We had to finish the discussion with only the prefect to help us.'

I gasped out loud, there at the breakfast table. I couldn't help it. Miss Hopkins's alibi, which had been so secure all the way through our investigation, had just been smashed to pieces. She had been down at school at the time of the murder. All her suspicious behaviour suddenly began to look rather sinister.

Daisy must have been as shocked as I was, but she only blinked. 'Miss Hopkins went back down to school on Monday evening?' she asked.

'Oh yes,' said Clementine, through a half-chewed mouthful of toast. 'Honestly, we were all furious about it. Can you imagine?'

The rest of the table made sympathetic noises. I wanted to jump up and down and shriek like Beanie. *Miss Hopkins might be the murderer!* What if she had been afraid that The One might leave her for Miss Bell, just the way he had left Miss Bell for her? She was very strong too (I thought of her swinging a hockey stick in Games) – she could easily have shoved Miss Bell off that balcony. I couldn't decide if I were pleased that my suspicions about Miss Hopkins might still be proven right, or frustrated to have our case made more messy . . . or even frightened; but I could tell that Daisy was simply annoyed.

'Why do you care if Miss Hopkins doesn't have an alibi?' I asked as we walked down to school. 'If she's got a motive and she's been behaving extremely oddly, why shouldn't she be a suspect?'

Daisy glared at me. 'You *know* why!' she said. 'Because she didn't do it, I know she didn't. And now we have to rule her out all over again. It's simply not tidy!'

'You only want to clear her name because you like her and you don't want her to have done it!'

'I don't see what's wrong with that!'

'Daisy, you can't be a proper detective if you don't follow the clues!' I said. 'What if she *did* do it?'

'She didn't! Anyway, I'm the President of the society. Have you forgotten?'

'What does that matter? I thought you said that I

was the cleverest person you knew in the whole school?'

'Apart from me! And *I* say that I don't think Miss Hopkins did it!'

We glared at each other.

'Well, you can do what you want,' said Daisy at last. 'Follow Miss Hopkins as well as Miss Parker this morning, if it'll make you happy. And you can do The One and Miss Lappet too, just for being so difficult. *I'm* going to follow Miss Tennyson.'

'All right, I *will* follow Miss Hopkins,' I said angrily, thinking how absolutely infuriating Daisy could be at times. 'Just you see . . . I'll follow Miss Hopkins and all the others and I'll show you what a good detective I am.'

'If you *must*,' said Daisy with a sigh. 'But when I discover that Miss Tennyson did it, don't say I didn't warn you.'

We both stormed through Old Wing Entrance.

7

Unfortunately, it was impossible to ignore Daisy and her annoying ideas. By the time Prayers was over, her séance story was all over the school. Miss Bell, everyone was telling each other, had not been kidnapped at all. She had been *murdered*.

It was very strange hearing other people say it, and for some reason it made me even more cross. It was *our* case, and Daisy had given it away to the rest of Deepdean.

The only way to show Daisy that she was going about the investigation the wrong way, though, was to concentrate on my own detective work. So after Prayers, when I saw Miss Lappet and Miss Parker heading to the mistresses' common room, I joined a line of second formers following Miss Hopkins. Miss Hopkins bounced along cheerfully and even patted a shrimp on the back – once again, she seemed far too happy. But was I just being prejudiced against her?

As I was wondering this, though, The One came striding round the corner in the other direction. He saw Miss Hopkins, and his face turned a deep, shameful shade of red. Miss Hopkins stopped so quickly her hair bounced, and she made a funny, shrill noise, like someone killing a mouse. The second formers stared between the two of them in fascination, and I was fascinated too. Was this behaviour evidence of some guilty secret? Just then the bell for the beginning of lessons rang, and I ran for our form room.

I bumped into Daisy just outside.

'I followed Miss Tennyson to the mistresses' lavs,' said Daisy coolly. 'She's hidden in there, and of course I can't get in, but I can hear her crying. It's extremely suspicious.'

'Miss Hopkins is being suspicious too,' I said. 'She saw The One and she went all *funny*.'

Daisy, I could see, was not interested in the slightest.

I spent the rest of the morning feeling as though I was trying to be in twenty places at once. Shadowing one person, let alone four, is an unexpectedly sweaty business. Between each lesson I went rushing about, trying to keep Miss Hopkins, The One, Miss Parker and Miss Lappet in sight at all times, and trying not to pant too heavily while I was doing it.

Miss Hopkins continued to be enormously cheerful, and to skip about the school like a bouncy ball. As she did so, I became grimly sure that she must be doing it on purpose. She did not run into The One again all morning, but to *me*, that one meeting had proved enough.

Miss Parker was far easier to follow – and, I had to admit, much more obviously disturbed by something. She stalked about scowling terribly and dragging her hands through her hair. Was she upset because of what had happened on Monday evening (I was nearly certain that she must at least have argued with Miss Bell), or was there something more to it? Was she worried by the new rumours?

Miss Lappet moved slowly, peering down at girls after she had nearly tripped over them. Her hair didn't look as though she had brushed it that morning, and once again her cardigan was mis-buttoned over her bosom. I realized that she had been showing signs of this sort of thing for days – ever since Tuesday, in fact. What was wrong with her? I knew she was doing the secretarying for Miss Griffin that Miss Bell usually did, but surely that extra work could not have been enough to tip her over the edge?

At bunbreak, Miss Hopkins and Miss Lappet went to ground again in the mistresses' common room. Miss Parker, though, swept straight past and on down

Library corridor. I chased her small figure in its jumper and brown skirt as she wove between groups of girls, and then hung back, just in time to see her climb the steps to The One's cubby door, knock on it and step inside.

Here was something interesting.

I edged through a crowd of second-form shrimps, checked my wristwatch as though I was waiting for someone, sighed deeply and plumped down onto the top step. Staring ahead of me vaguely, I let my head lean backwards until it was resting as near as possible to the door hinge. For added camouflage I pulled *Swallows and Amazons* out of my bag and opened it on my lap as though I was reading. Then I let my eyes unfocus from the text and listened with all my might to what was happening in the room behind me.

The first thing I heard was The One. If it had been anyone else, I would have said he sounded angry.

'. . . don't know why you think I have anything to do with this,' he was saying.

'I *know* you do!' said Miss Parker, cutting across him. She really was angry, nearly raving. 'Joan *told* me – she said that you and she—'

(For a moment I wondered what someone called *Joan* had to do with anything, and then I remembered that it was Miss Bell's first name.)

'I tell you you're wrong!' The One *did* shout then, and I jumped and had to pretend I had cramp.

'No,' said Miss Parker, and her voice went much quieter, so that I could barely hear her. 'I know she went back to you, and I want you to admit it. You must give me—'

There was a heavy thump. 'I will give you *nothing*!' shouted The One. 'You have no right to ask! Get out of my office at once!'

'I shall!' Miss Parker screamed back. 'But you'll be sorry! I'll come back and— Oh!'

Trying to look as interested in *Swallows and Amazons* as I could, I hurriedly bumped down the stairs. When Miss Parker shoved the door open a few seconds later I was sitting innocently on the bottom step, engrossed in my book.

I needn't have bothered. She pushed past without noticing me and stormed off down the corridor, nearly crashing into Miss Hopkins, who happened to be coming the other way, her hair bouncing more than ever. Was she coming to see The One? I hung back to see where she would go – and sure enough, she began to climb the steps to The One's cubby.

Just then, though, the bell to end bunbreak rang. Cursing school bells, I stuffed *Swallows and Amazons* back into my bag and walked away. What did what I had just heard mean? Were Miss Hopkins and The One working

together? Had Miss Parker discovered something awful
about them? Was she even planning to *blackmail* them
now that she had heard the new rumours? Off I went
to History, thinking that at last I had something really
important to tell Daisy, something so good that even she
could not ignore it.

8

I should have known that Daisy would find a way to foil me. She rushed into History when we were already standing up for Miss Lappet to come in.

'Good of you to grace us with your presence, Daisy,' said Miss Lappet, who was looking just as flustered and mis-buttoned as she had earlier. Also, I could tell from close to, she had a sickly after-dinner smell wafting about her. Next to me, Kitty mouthed to Beanie, *Tippling again.*

'Sorry, Miss Lappet,' said Daisy, pretending to be contrite. 'It won't happen again, Miss Lappet. Miss Lappet?'

'What, Daisy?' asked Miss Lappet, and steadied herself with both hands on her desk.

'Miss Lappet, I was wondering if you were the one who went round collecting lost property on Monday evening. You see, I've lost my very special pen, and—'

Miss Lappet sighed windily. 'Enough, Daisy,' she said. 'You do speak loudly sometimes. As it happens, that evening Miss Bell was in charge of confiscations and lost property.' (The whole form stiffened at the mention of Miss Bell's name.) 'Not that she ever handed any in before she resigned. I was in Miss Griffin's office, discussing important matters, for the entire evening.'

'Oh,' said Daisy, flashing a private, triumphant look at me. 'So – you were there the entire evening?'

'Good grief, Daisy!' snapped Miss Lappet, clutching her forehead. 'You never listen, do you? Yes, I was there the whole evening. And what does this have to do with your pen?'

So, I thought to myself, *that did for Miss Lappet.* I had to admit that it was neat of Daisy to get her alibi like that. But afterwards, it was no good me even attempting to send a note. Miss Lappet kept her eyes focused (with a slight effort) on Daisy through the entire lesson. I had no chance to let Daisy know about the argument I had overheard between Miss Parker and The One, and so when we went on to Music I was the only member of the Detective Society who knew that we had a new reason to watch him.

It was a good thing I did. Wrinkling his handsome brow, The One barely managed to hold a tune on the piano, confused Kitty with Lavinia, forgot to set us prep, fell over a tambourine and then wished us a good evening – at one o'clock in the afternoon. Even Beanie noticed that something was wrong.

'P'raps he's in mourning for Miss Bell,' she said to us on the way out of Old Wing Entrance at lunch time.

Unfortunately, Miss Lappet happened to be passing by, and she was still cross.

'Beanie!' she snapped. Beanie froze in horror. 'Enough! If I hear you repeating any more foolish and baseless gossip it'll be the whole third form in detention for all of next week. Am I clear?'

'Yes, Miss Lappet.' Beanie gulped. 'Sorry, Miss Lappet.'

We walked up to House very quietly, in case we spread any more rumours by mistake, and Beanie stayed with us all the way . . . Yet again, I had no chance to talk to Daisy.

In a way, though, this was a good thing. I was free to think about The One without any interruptions or contradictions. He had shown exactly the sort of behaviour that you might expect of someone who had just been blackmailed. The more I thought about it, the more I decided that there was no other explanation for the row I had overheard. The One knew something about Miss Bell's murder – from what I had witnessed, it seemed likely that he and Miss Hopkins *both* knew something about it – and Miss Parker knew that they knew. But could The One really be a murderer? Perhaps he was just covering for Miss Hopkins's crime. Was that why she had gone hurrying down to school on Monday night? So much for Daisy being sure Miss Hopkins was innocent!

I felt quite triumphant about my deductions. At last it was *me* who had come up with the important clue, and Daisy who would have to follow along behind.

But it was Daisy who cornered me.

'Come with me,' she ordered, as soon as we had finished lunch. 'I've got the plan ready at last.'

'Daisy, I have to tell you what I heard at bunbreak. I think Miss Parker is blackmailing The One. Honestly! I think he and Miss Hopkins—'

'Shh,' said Daisy. 'Dorm.'

The dorm room was empty when we arrived. We made straight for my bed and sat down facing one another.

'Daisy,' I said again, as soon as the door closed on us. 'You've got to listen. I think Miss Hopkins and The One are in it together. We know that he was down at school, and that she came back halfway through hockey practice. One of them could have done it, or maybe it was both of them, and then Miss Parker found out somehow and now she's blackmailing them! Miss Parker went into The One's study at bunbreak and I heard them arguing.'

'Oh, Hazel,' said Daisy. I could hardly believe it. She was dismissing me. 'How do you know she was *blackmailing* him? Did you hear her actually ask him for money?'

'No,' I said. 'But—'

'Exactly. She's furious about his past with Miss Bell – we know that already. She must have just gone to confront him about it again. Anyway, it hardly matters. I've got something much more important to show you!'

She dug about in the depths of her book bag and then pulled out a little glass bottle. She waved it at me, beaming as though I ought to be particularly impressed. I wasn't. I wanted to shout at her. She *had* to listen to me.

'What is it this time?' I asked crossly.

'Ipecac,' said Daisy. 'I got it from Alice Murgatroyd.' Then, seeing my look, she said, 'Oh, honestly, where did you come from? Every nursery has it. Nanny used to make us take it whenever we'd eaten something we oughtn't. It makes you awfully sick. It's exactly what we need.'

I did not understand, and I was not in the mood to try. I was still cross. Why was Daisy's idiotic idea more important than my perfectly good clue?

'Don't you see?' asked Daisy, still chugging along on her own triumphant train of thought. 'If we're going to go hunting for clues about Miss Bell, we need to get into the school when we can snoop about without any of the mistresses or masters wondering what we're up to – and more importantly, without the murderer noticing us. That means at night, and the easiest way to do that is to get admitted to San. If we take this we won't need to pretend at all – we'll be sick everywhere and Minny will have to keep us in San overnight. Then all we need to do is wait until she falls asleep and we can go wherever we like.'

'But won't everywhere be locked?' I objected.

'Not if I steal Jones's spare keys, you chump,' said Daisy.

'All right,' I said. 'All right, I'll do it. But only if you explain why Miss Hopkins and The One aren't guilty of the murder.'

'Because Miss Tennyson did it, of course,' said Daisy. 'Oh, I haven't told you my findings from today yet, have I?'

'No,' I said furiously. 'No, you haven't.'

'Well, she's an absolute wreck. She might as well be wandering the corridors muttering, *Out, damned spot*! I think our séance rumour has spooked her. While I was following her one of the Big Girls tapped her on the shoulder and she *shrieked*. But here's the important bit: there I was, minding my own business in an opportune listening place on Library corridor, when Miss Griffin came up to Miss Tennyson. "Miss Tennyson," she said, "I need to talk to you. You haven't quite finished helping me with that little project of ours. You were so late to my office on Monday evening that we barely got a thing done."

"'Yes, but I made up for it on Tuesday and Wednesday," said Miss Tennyson nervously.

"'Ah, but not quite," replied Miss Griffin. "There's still a bit of work that needs to be finished." Honestly, Hazel, Miss Tennyson went as white as a sheet. She was *shaking.* "Can we perhaps schedule another session?" asked Miss Griffin. "There's just a little more work I'd like you to do – perhaps this evening?"'

'So what?' I asked. 'Miss Tennyson and Miss Griffin are going to mark books together after school today. That doesn't have anything to do with the murder.'

'Hazel,' said Daisy, rolling her eyes, 'sometimes you are a bit stupid. Miss Griffin had an appointment with Miss Tennyson on *Monday* night, but Miss Tennyson was *late.* Miss Tennyson takes English Soc until five twenty, so the appointment must have been for after that – for *exactly the time when Miss Bell was being murdered.* And I'm sure the way Miss Tennyson behaved when Miss Griffin mentioned Monday was a sign. Hazel, it's her guilty conscience! She must have done it!'

'If you say so,' I said. I was still annoyed. Here was Daisy again, sure that *her* idea was the important one.

'Oh, Hazel, don't be like that,' said Daisy, butting her head against my shoulder and staring at me wide-eyed. 'Hazel, Hazel, Hazel, Hazel, *Hazel*—'

'Ow!' I said, scowling. 'I'm not smiling.'

'Yes you *are*,' said Daisy, leaping up off the bed and grabbing hold of my arm. 'Come on, come on, let's go downstairs before Matron wonders where we've got to. Oh, and meet me in the cloakroom before French and we'll take this disgusting stuff.' She brandished the bottle of ipecac at me, stuffed it into her book bag and galloped out of the dorm.

9

Daisy can be really insufferable sometimes, but I suppose, given what happened on my first night at Deepdean, I shouldn't be surprised.

After our first meeting on the games fields I came back to House, shivering and pink with cold, to the tall and chilly walls of the second-form dorm room. I sat on my strict grey bed and stared about me at the rows of identical bedsteads and the dismally scratchy and grey bedspreads. I was quite upset by the sight of it, and I remember wondering whether Deepdean might not be doing so well for itself after all. (I had not yet discovered that in England, the way of showing that you are very rich is to pretend that you are very poor and cannot afford things like heating or new shoes.)

One of the maids had unpacked my trunk, and all my things were folded up in the chipped chest of drawers next to my bed. The trunk itself was standing open and empty on the carpet, still with customs stamps all over it, and I looked at it and felt just as empty and out of place. The other girls in the dorm were ignoring me, huddled into a group at the other end of the room. Then one of them, the girl with the long gold hair who had run into me earlier, turned abruptly and made her way over to me. The others all followed in a gaggle and grouped themselves behind her, like a pack of crows or a monster with four heads and eight hard, staring eyes.

'Hallo, foreign girl,' said Daisy – for, of course, that golden-haired girl was Daisy.

'Hallo,' I said shyly.

All the girls giggled. 'She can speak English!' someone I later learned was Kitty whispered. 'Lavinia, you owe me five bob.'

'Foreign girl,' said Daisy, 'we're going to play a game. We've decided to let you join in – and that's unusual for us.' My heart jumped. 'It's a test, really – we want to see who can stick it out longest in that trunk. Kitty thinks no one could do it for more than ten minutes, but *I* think it'd be easy. And we want *you* to go first. It is your trunk, after all. What do you say?'

Today, I can't think how I could ever have fallen for it. But at the time I was simply excited to think that I might be making friends already – and that someone so beautiful should want *me* to be friends with her. So I nodded.

'All right, then,' said Daisy, 'get in.' And while the rest of the dorm watched breathlessly, I stepped into my trunk and crouched down with my arms about my knees.

'Now,' said Daisy, 'we're going to shut the lid. Otherwise it wouldn't be a proper test, would it? Lavinia, you time her. Remember, foreign girl, you've got to stick it out for as long as you can. All right?'

I nodded again, squeezing my hands together. I hate the dark, and I hated it even more then, but I didn't want to say so to someone so obviously faultless.

Daisy bent down over me, so close I could feel her breath warm against my forehead. 'Enjoy, foreign girl,' she hissed, and then the lid of the trunk slammed shut and I was left in the dark. I heard giggles, a clicking noise, then squeals of laughter and the thump of running feet, which faded away and became part of a larger clatter of feet going down the stairs. A gong boomed somewhere below me, the feet sped up in a rush, and then at last they died away.

House was very quiet. Crouching in my trunk, I began to suspect that something was not right. I had been told that the gong meant a meal, and I knew I must never be late to a meal. And I was hungry. But, I thought, I had also been told to stick it out, and so that was what I would do. I was in England, and in England, I knew, you kept quiet and endured things.

So that is what I did. It took Matron three hours to find me, and when she finally did, she was almost frying with rage. She asked me who had been responsible – but, of course, I knew I could not tell her without being a rat. For a week I had to spend my lunch breaks sitting beside her and sewing up holes in socks – but it was worth it when Daisy clapped me on the back and said, with admiration in her voice, 'Not bad, foreign girl.'

I suppose, in a way, I have been getting into trunks for Daisy ever since, without stopping to ask why. This is the first time I have wondered if it is really all worth it.

PART FIVE

WE CARRY OUT SOME DARING NIGHT-TIME DETECTION

1

On Friday afternoon I arrived in the cloakroom rather before Daisy. I had decided, for the time being, to forgive her – at least until I had seen more of her plan. I was hunched up behind a thick grey row of coats, rubbing my ankle, and was just beginning to feel nervous about what we were about to do when I heard Daisy's voice say, 'Psst! Hazel!'

'Here!' I whispered, sticking my head round the end of my coat rack.

'Well lurked, Watson,' said Daisy, sitting down next to me with a *thump*. She pulled the little bottle out of her bag with a flourish and held it up in front of us. 'Now, are you ready to begin investigating?'

We both looked at the bottle. I was quite ready to investigate, but not sure whether I wanted to go to San first.

'We must be careful not to take too much,' said Daisy.

'I remember Nanny saying that it could be dangerous.'

'How much is too much?' I asked.

'I've no idea,' said Daisy cheerfully. 'We'll just have to swig it and hope. Well, bottoms up!'

She took a gulp, made a face and handed the bottle to me. I sipped at it nervously. It tasted sticky and sugary-sweet, not at all the way I thought it would.

'Now water from the taps, quick,' Daisy said. I hurried after her and drank. Afterwards my mouth still felt gluey with sugar.

'What do we do now?' I asked.

'We wait. It shouldn't take too long. Don't worry, it's not so bad.'

2

That was a lie.

I had barely sat down in French before my stomach began to make the most extraordinary jumps and heaves inside me. I clapped my hand over my mouth in horror.

'Oh, Mamzelle,' cried Daisy dramatically from next to me, 'I think I'm going to be sick!'

And she was, spectacularly. After that, so was I, but since most people were already crowding round Daisy it was not so noticeable. We were both rushed to San, leaving nasty splotches behind us as we ran, and when we arrived Nurse Minn took one look at us, stuck our heads over two buckets and left us to it.

'At least we're missing Deportment,' I said between heaves, an hour later. I hate Deportment, which is an hour of walking about with piles of books on your head.

'I don't mind Deportment,' said Daisy hollowly from within her bucket.

'I know you don't. *I* do,' I said, and heaved again.

But even missing Deportment was little comfort. I heaved for hours, all the way through tea and dinner, without wanting them at all. My stomach felt as though it had been turned inside out.

'I must say, this is rather worse than I remembered,' gasped Daisy. 'What I wouldn't give to stop so I could have a bun.'

The thought of that made me heave again, and then Daisy heaved too. It was all very miserable, and I decided in the middle of a particularly nasty retch that after this we deserved to find some really excellent clues.

'The two of you had better stay the night, I think,' said Minny, coming in to look at us. 'I've some things you can use to sleep in. Goodness, you did eat something that disagreed with you, didn't you?'

At last, after hours of being ill, the heaving stopped, and I was able to get up and put on the pyjamas Minny had left out for me. They managed to be both long in the legs and tight in the waist, and I saw in the San mirror that I looked like an enormous, ill baby, with a pale round face and ugly damp hair. Daisy's pyjamas, of course, fitted her perfectly, and being sick had only made her cheeks pink and her eyes bright, like a nice china doll.

I dragged myself into my cool white-sheeted San bed. I felt as though someone had squeezed me through a mangle. All I wanted to do was sleep, for years and years.

Daisy, though, had different ideas.

'As soon as Minny's asleep we can begin,' she whispered to me from the next bed, sounding not at all like someone who had just been sick for six hours straight.

'Yes, Daisy,' I said, and I turned over and went to sleep.

3

It only seemed a moment later that I was woken up by someone shaking me hard. I opened my eyes to see Daisy's shadowy face looming over mine.

'Get up, you lazy thing!' she hissed. 'It's time!'

Grumbling, and still feeling mangled inside, I got up and pulled on the dressing gown that Minny had helpfully laid across the foot of my bed.

'I already have Jones's spare keys,' said Daisy, dangling them before me. 'I went and picked them up while you were waiting in the cloakroom. He never notices they're gone – I've taken them heaps of times before.'

'How nice for you,' I said. I was still struggling not to argue.

'Sourpuss,' said Daisy, sticking out her tongue. 'Don't be. Let's get on with it.'

It was quite easy to escape San. We unlocked the

main door and crept out, holding the torches that Daisy had hidden for us in the bottom of her bag.

'Where do we go now?' I glanced about the dark corridor and couldn't stop myself shivering. For the moment it was empty, and we were alone, but what would we do if the murderer – made nervous by Daisy's rumour – appeared?

'We're off to the Gym, of course,' said Daisy. 'Scene of the crime. Careful – keep your torch low. We can't afford to have someone notice the light.'

I shivered again, but off we went.

4

The skin on the back of my neck prickled. We were heading towards the Gym, to the place where the murder had happened. In the dark night, it was not only the murderer I found myself afraid of – all my silly, babyish fears appeared again, stronger than ever. Verity's ghost still lurked in the Gym, and who knew whether Miss Bell's had joined her? I stayed just behind Daisy and did not look round. I kept my eyes fixed on the little puddle of moving light cast by her torch, because I was terrified that it was too bright. Would someone else notice it?

At last we arrived at the door to the Gym, but instead of going out onto the floor, Daisy turned right and started up the steep flight of wooden stairs that led to the balcony. Soon the empty Gym was stretched out below us.

I didn't like it. I am not fond of heights at the best of times, and the Gym at night was a horrid place. It was dim and murky, and black shadows crouched at its edges. This was how Miss Bell had seen it, I thought, just before she fell. The ground suddenly seemed very far below me, and the narrow balcony with its rows of wooden benches swayed in front of me.

'Why are we up here?' I asked, clutching the railing.

'Don't be slow, Hazel,' said Daisy. 'We're going to reconstruct the crime.'

'But we know what happened,' I said. 'Someone pushed Miss Bell off the balcony. You – you don't want . . . ?' For one dreadful second I actually thought that Daisy was asking me to jump off the balcony while she watched.

'Don't be a chump, Hazel,' said Daisy. 'We're not actually going to push anything off. Goodness! I want you to go downstairs and show me exactly where you found Miss Bell. I'll stay up here and look.'

I went back down extremely thankfully, but going into the Gym again made my skin crawl worse than ever. It was exactly the way it had been on Monday night – although, of course, without Miss Bell lying there. I went over to where I had found her and looked up to see Daisy peering down at me from the balcony. All I could see was her face with her blonde hair hanging down around it and her eyes staring at me. For a moment she looked horribly like my idea of Verity Abraham's ghost. My heart jumped.

'Are you ready?' Daisy called. 'How was she lying?'

'Her arm was back, like this,' I said, trying to demonstrate. 'And she was a bit curled up—'

'Oh, for heaven's sake,' said Daisy, 'lie down yourself and show me. I'll never be able to understand it otherwise.'

I did not like the idea at all. Pretending to be Miss Bell felt all wrong and quite horrible, but Daisy was glaring down at me and I knew there was nothing else for it. Reluctantly, I lay down on the wooden floor and stretched myself out in an imitation of Miss Bell's position. I closed my eyes and Daisy's torch flickered across my eyelids.

'Is that all right?' I asked after a while.

'Perfectly,' said Daisy from next to my ear. My eyes flew open. She was crouching down next to me, staring up at the wall and the edge of the balcony above.

'This was exactly how she was lying?' Daisy asked, peering at me.

'Exactly,' I said. 'So?'

'So, from the way she was lying, she must have gone over the balcony railing backwards.'

'She was facing the murderer,' I said, shuddering. I had a sudden image of a pair of hands reaching out and shoving Miss Bell off the balcony.

'Exactly, Hazel. So, to continue with our reconstruction. You've just murdered Miss Bell. She's lying on the floor, dead. What do you do next?'

'Find somewhere to hide the body,' I said.

'Yes indeed. The fact that the body was still there when you came in does rather suggest that the deed had only just been done. And the fact that the body was gone when we came back again – well, that suggests that the body and the murderer were hidden somewhere very close indeed. They really *must* have been in the Cupboard, like we said – and, golly, that must have been where the murderer hid when you first came in too!'

My mouth went dry. I remembered running into the Gym. It had seemed so empty and quiet – and the murderer had been just a few feet away from me!

'But the body couldn't have *stayed* there!' I said.

Daisy rolled her eyes. 'Of course it couldn't,' she said. 'The girls changing in there before first lesson on Tuesday morning would've noticed a *dead body* among the gym slips. But all the same, it *must* have been used as the temporary hiding place. Nothing else makes sense. And remember that smash-up yesterday? I'm sure I'm right that it was caused by that trolley, the one that Jones keeps in there. So all in all, the Cupboard is crucial to this case. We can't put off looking inside it any more. Come on!'

She dug her fingers into my arm and dragged me, stumbling, across the floor towards the musty storeroom. I felt clammy and cold all over, as though I was going to be sick again. I did not want to look in the Cupboard.

But Daisy left me no choice. She threw open the door and flashed her torch about inside. I had to admit that it looked just the same as it always did – spiderwebbed white walls and piled-up mounds of fencing whites, badminton rackets, croquet mallets, calisthenics mats and gym slips – but all the same I was terrified.

Daisy leaped straight for the trolley, which was standing innocently beside the door, draped in discarded clothes, and began throwing things off it with frantic excitement. I turned away and dug through what I hoped was a harmless old pile of gym slips, of the sort that we hardly wear any more.

Unfortunately, the pile tipped over and spilled across the floor, and I saw that one of the gym slips had a long, dark smear all down its front. I shone my torch on it, and it came up rusty in the light. While I was still standing there, hoping that what I was seeing was not really true, Daisy gave a yelp.

'View-halloo!' she cried. 'As suspected, blood on the trolley! I say, Hazel, *look*!'

I turned round, holding up the bloodied gym slip.

5

Daisy could not understand why I was not more excited.

'Watson!' she cried, poking me jubilantly in the ribs. 'The game's afoot! We're closing in!'

I bit my lip. The Case of the Murder of Miss Bell was feeling far too real. Miss Bell really was dead and was never coming back. I was holding a gym slip with real blood on it – the gym slip that the murderer must have used to mop Miss Bell's blood off the Gym floor – and Daisy had found the trolley the murderer had used to transport Miss Bell's body to its hiding place.

But Daisy was still galloping on, as excited about this case as she had been about The Case of The Mysterious Tuck Box Thief – as though Miss Bell was just another missing bag of bull's eyes. 'We're close!' she cried. 'We're very close! We've got the scent, and now we must run with it. Here's the trolley, and a bloodied gym slip, and here *isn't* Miss Bell's body. So, where was she moved to? The murderer must have stowed the Bell somewhere at school between Monday evening and Tuesday night, when they came back to move it to a safer hiding place, away from the school. So now we need to be clever; we need to put ourselves into the mind of the killer. If you had a body to hide *in* Deepdean, what would you do with it?'

'I wouldn't kill anyone in the first place,' I said.

'All right, *don't* be clever,' said Daisy. 'Think. It needs to be somewhere safe, and it needs to be somewhere secure.'

'That doesn't sound much like anywhere in Deepdean,' I said. Honestly, I couldn't think of a single place that would fit. A safe and secure place in Deepdean? If I'd been in a rude mood – instead of feeling frightened – I'd have said, *Not likely*.

Daisy frowned. 'Yes, I know,' she said. 'It doesn't, does it? Not for years, anyway. *Years!* Ever since they closed up the—'

She froze. I could see an idea occurring to her, like a firework going off in her head.

'Hazel! We've been the most utter chumps! Imagine us not thinking of *that*! Oh, I could kick myself!' And without any more explanation, she took my hand and dragged me out into the Gym again, so that I had to gallop after her or fall over.

'Of what?' I asked, gasping as we jolted along. '*What?*'

'You'll see!' shouted Daisy. 'Come on, come on, quick!'

She towed me out into the corridor, then immediately dragged me left into a little passageway behind the Hall. When Deepdean was first built there used to be an underground tunnel between the Hall and Old Wing, so that when it rained girls could go to Prayers without getting wet. It was bricked up long ago, though, when Library corridor was built, and now that little passageway only leads to a locked door.

At last I understood where Daisy was taking me.

'Oh!' I said, stopping so quickly that Daisy nearly jerked my wrist off before she noticed.

'*Now* do you see?' asked Daisy, wheeling round and letting go of me. 'It *has* to be! There's nowhere else even half so perfect.'

'But no one can get into it!'

'Jones can, and anyone who knows the school at all could take his spare keys, just like I did. I think this is really it, Hazel! We've found it!'

I thought of Miss Bell again. 'You're sure she's not still down there?' I asked uncomfortably.

'I've told you she isn't. She's been moved out of the school by now,' said Daisy. 'But even if she is – well, I've seen lots of dead animals and they're not so bad. They just lie there.' I nearly reminded her that I had seen Miss Bell's body quite recently, and it had not been like a dead animal at all. But Daisy was already trying Jones's keys in the door. I thought it would be difficult to unlock, but when Daisy found the right key it turned with a neat little well-oiled *click* and the door swung inwards.

'See?' asked Daisy smugly. 'Someone's been here recently.'

She flashed her torch into the open doorway and we saw brickwork, broken bits of cobweb and steps going down into darkness. They were dusty, but instead of lying in a smooth layer, the dust had been scuffed up and smudged about, and in the middle it had been rubbed away altogether in a sort of snaky track.

Daisy took my hand and squeezed it. I squeezed back. Her palm was cool and dry, and I remember being terribly worried she might notice how much I was sweating. She said nothing, though, and we went down into the tunnel hand in hand, both of us shining our torches into the dark.

'Do look at this floor,' said Daisy, stepping daintily through the dust. 'That drag mark must be from Miss Bell.'

She sounded so casual about it! I flashed my torch around the scuff mark, trying to avoid it, and that is when I caught sight of the sideways print of a shoe, just clear of the track. 'Oh!' I said, pointing, and Daisy sprang at it with a yelp of excitement.

Drawing a bit of string and a pencil from the pocket of her dressing gown, Daisy crouched down over the print. I knelt next to her, shining my torch at it while she laid the string over the print and deftly marked it off with the pencil. It was the print of a flat shoe, and it was very long. When Daisy held up the string in the glare of my torch, it looked longer than ever.

'A man!' I exclaimed. 'The One, it must be! Didn't I tell you he had something to do with it?'

Daisy looked at me pityingly. 'Don't you ever notice anything, Hazel? This print isn't from a man's shoe at all. Look at the heel, and the toe. Ugly as sin, but it's made for a woman, and I know exactly which one.'

'Who?' I asked. 'Miss Bell?'

'Hazel,' said Daisy, 'that is the stupidest thing I have ever heard you say. I shall pretend I didn't hear it. Haven't you ever noticed those boats of Miss Tennyson's?'

My stomach lurched. That was exactly what I had *not* wanted to find – real evidence to back up Daisy's Miss Tennyson theory.

'*Miss Tennyson?*'

'Just you look at her shoes tomorrow. They're simply enormous. She only has two pairs too. This is from one of her blue monstrosities. *You* know, the ones with the pointless bows.'

'But – someone else might have put on her shoes?'
I suggested. I had felt so *sure* it must have been
The One.

'Oh, don't be an ass, Hazel. That sort of thing is too
silly to happen in real life. Unless you think they crept
into her boarding house and stole her shoes just to wear
them in a passageway that no one ever uses?'

I blushed. I felt like an idiot, and I was glad it was
so dark.

'We ought to get on,' said Daisy, getting up and
tucking the curl of string back into her pocket. 'We can't
be away from San too long. Besides, we need something
else to prove what happened. That footprint's no good
on its own.'

She started off down the tunnel again, walking
carefully along the drag line in the dust, and I
followed her.

That night, everything seemed to be going Daisy's
way. She wanted another clue, and she found exactly
what she was hoping for. I heard her give an exclama-
tion, and saw her flash her torch onto a little wisp of
whiteness that had been caught low down on a rough
part of the tunnel's brick wall. It was a little scrap of
white fabric, plain and coarse, and we both recognized
it at once.

'This is from the Bell's lab coat!' whispered Daisy.
'Now we *know* she was left here for a while. Oh, and

look!' When she had rushed forward to snatch up the bit of coat she had stirred up the dust on the floor, and now something glittered in the torchlight. 'An earring! A lovely long gold one. Clues rain down upon us! *This* isn't from Miss Bell.'

Grudgingly, I shook my head. Miss Bell would never have worn a delicate gold earring like the one Daisy was holding.

'It must be Miss Tennyson's,' said Daisy.

'It might be almost anyone's,' I pointed out. Although Miss Bell didn't wear earrings, almost all of the other mistresses did. This earring was a pretty gold double teardrop – I could quite well imagine Miss Lappet, Miss Parker or Miss Hopkins all wearing something like it, as well as Miss Tennyson.

'It looks quite new,' said Daisy, examining it. 'Good quality too. You can't prove it's *not* Tennyson's, and if you put it with the shoe, things begin to look awfully bad for her.'

I wanted to protest that she was still not being open-minded, but the sight of all that evidence kept me quiet. Daisy was right. I could *not* prove that Miss Tennyson was not the owner of the earring, while Daisy might well be able to match that string to the length of her shoes. I told myself that it did not matter who had done it, as long as we unmasked them, but I still had a nagging worry in the back of my mind.

We went down the rest of the tunnel, but found no more clues, and, much to my relief, no body either. Miss Bell had gone.

I wrapped the string, the bit of lab coat and the earring in the stained gym slip, while Daisy held the torches, and we began to creep back to San. I thought that the night's adventures were over.

They weren't.

We had just turned into Library corridor when something flashed away to our right, down New Wing corridor.

'Daisy!' I hissed. 'Hold the torches down! They're reflecting on something, look!'

'Don't be stupid, Hazel, I *am* holding— Hazel. Hazel, *that isn't a reflection from our torches.*'

All the hairs on my neck stood up in horror. She was right. That light was not being made by us at all. It was from a different torch, being held by someone walking down New Wing corridor. There was someone else prowling around Deepdean in the middle of the night.

'Oh Lord, Hazel,' gasped Daisy, flicking off our torches, plunging us into darkness and making the other light seem suddenly much larger and more menacing. 'Run!'

I did not need to be told twice. We ran, scuffling and bumping into each other, our bare feet slapping on the marble tiles. I was shaking. The murderer was here, in Deepdean, now! Because, of course, it *had* to be the murderer. Had they seen our light? Worse, had they seen *us*? I'd thought we were in danger before, but it was nothing to the danger we were in now.

We ran all the way back to San, as though the murderer was panting at our heels, and when Daisy dragged the main San door to and locked it, my knees gave out beneath me, and I slumped down on the floor. It was only then that I noticed that my ankle was hurting fearfully again.

'Up!' said Daisy firmly. 'Wash! Or Minny will smell a rat.'

So we went to the washroom to scrub off our filthy hands and feet, and then we crept back to our beds. I thought I should never get to sleep. I thought I might never sleep again. I said so to Daisy and she said, 'Lord, I know!' and then began to snore. Even though I was frightened, somehow I must have slept as well, because the next thing I remember was Minny knocking on our open door and saying, 'Rise and shine, girls! How are we feeling this morning?'

6

We sat up, and Minny felt our foreheads and looked down our throats with that flat stick nurses always have. Then she told us we seemed far better today.

It was Saturday. At Deepdean, we have lessons on Saturday morning – really, we do – but luckily Minny did not let us out of San until the morning was halfway through. Daisy managed to wangle us a perfectly heavenly San breakfast before we went, too – three slices of toast instead of two, strawberry jam instead of marmalade *and* a mug of cocoa, and we were let out of San just in time for bunbreak. It was almost enough to make me forget what had happened the night before.

Almost, but not quite.

'Oh!' Beanie squealed when she saw us, moving back so we could slip into the biscuit queue. 'I was so worried!'

'She was sure you were dying,' said Kitty, putting an arm round Beanie's shoulder.

'I was not!'

'Jammy of you, getting out of Latin like that,' said Lavinia as she pushed the shrimp in front of her out of the way. 'Some people have all the luck.'

'We missed Deportment, though,' said Daisy regretfully. 'Oh, I wish those shrimps would hurry up! I'm starving.'

Once we had collected our biscuits – only squashed fly on Saturdays, which I think is hardly worth it, though Daisy loves them – Daisy and I shook off the rest of the third form and went in search of Jones, to make certain that our night-time quest had gone undetected, and to return the borrowed keys. We found him out by the flowerbeds, telling off one of the gardeners.

'Hello, Miss Daisy – and . . . ah,' he said when he caught sight of us. 'Feeling better today?'

'Nothing ever gets past you, Jones,' said Daisy in her best admiring voice. 'However did you know we were ill?'

'Who do you think mopped up after you? Nasty mess you made. Feels like I've been cleaning up messes all week, though, so yours wasn't so much of a bother.'

'Oh, have you?' asked Daisy. She sounded terribly sympathetic, but I could feel her arm tense up next to mine. Had we left dirty footprints behind us?

Jones huffed down his nose. 'Indeed. Those smashed windows were the worst of it, but all week I've been finding little things out of place. This morning I come in and everything's a mess in New Wing, the Gym cupboard's all untidy and these flowerbeds have been turned over. Look at them! All scratched up and the flowers ruined. We only put the new winter beds in on Monday too. If it *is* those shrimps, they need a good talking to.'

'Poor Jones,' said Daisy. 'How awful for you. Here, look, you've dropped your keys.'

'It is awful,' said Jones forcefully, taking them from her without even looking. I admired Daisy's cunning all over again. 'Not that anyone else thinks of me. I complained to Miss Griffin again this morning and she told me it was nothing to worry about. Nothing! I ask you.'

The bell rang as he said that, and we had to run. We left him still scowling at his dirty flowerbeds.

'Good,' said Daisy, as soon as we were out of earshot. 'He doesn't know it was us.'

'But Daisy,' I said, 'it *wasn't* us. Not all of it! We messed about in the Gym cupboard, but we weren't anywhere near New Wing last night, were we? And we never went outside, so the mess in the flowerbeds wasn't us either. It must have been the murderer . . .'

Daisy stopped suddenly, her mouth open. 'Lord, I

know exactly what they were doing to make that mess! That earring we found – I bet they discovered they'd lost it, so they've been coming back in the evenings to hunt for it.'

She looked delighted. I still felt horrified at our narrow escape.

'Well, it's a good thing we got to it first,' said Daisy, making the best of things as usual. 'This is getting quite exciting, isn't it? Now come on, we'll be late for Prep.'

Saturday Prep is a Deepdean institution, something that is meant to be good for our character, like boiled vegetables and Games. We go into our form rooms and struggle away at all the week's undone work, which of course none of us except Daisy could ever finish – and she makes sure not to.

As luck would have it, we came into Prep to see that Miss Tennyson was taking it that day. I froze in the doorway, and Daisy had to kick me from behind to get me to move.

I realized that Miss Tennyson was staring at me. I also realized that we were so late that the only two seats left were the ones directly in front of her desk. I slid into the left-hand one, feeling as though her eyes were burning into the middle of my forehead. Was she really the murderer? I didn't want her to be. But there were her big blue shoes, peeping out at me from under the desk. I got a sinking feeling in my stomach, as if the ipecac sickness was coming back.

I tried to focus on my Latin translation. *The queen was in the woods*, I wrote. But, almost as though they were not under my control, my eyes kept sliding up off my work to stare at Miss Tennyson.

The third time I did it, I found her staring back at me. It gave me a nasty shock. Was Miss Tennyson remembering seeing our torchlight by the Gym? Did she know it had been us, and was she plotting to kill me and Daisy, as she had Miss Bell? I shuddered. But then I really looked at her, and what I saw surprised me. For a moment she did not look like an evil murderer at all, or even a mistress, but just someone who was terribly, terribly afraid. She had dark rings under her eyes, which were red-rimmed as though she had just been crying.

Was this what a guilty conscience looked like?

But just then there was a scuffle, a scraping noise and something thumped against my leg. I glanced down and saw – Daisy. She was wriggling across the wooden class-room floor between the desks, her hair in disarray and her arms outstretched. The marked bit of string was clutched in them, and she was inching determinedly towards Miss Tennyson's feet.

I looked up at Miss Tennyson in horror. What if she noticed that Daisy had gone from her desk next to me? What if she glanced down and saw what Daisy was doing? But she didn't. Her eyes were on the book she was reading, and she was crying again. Her tears scattered across the pages.

Meanwhile Daisy had reached her goal. The piece of string was stretched out against one of Miss Tennyson's shoes. It was exactly the right length. Daisy squirmed round triumphantly to look at me, and as she did so her hand bumped against Miss Tennyson's leg. Miss Tennyson jumped.

'Good grief!' she said, looking down at last. 'Daisy! Whatever are you doing?'

'Oh, Miss Tennyson—' said Daisy awkwardly, from the floor. 'Oh, Miss Tennyson – I'm feeling, er, most dreadfully strange. I think I might be sick. Hazel and I were frightfully ill last night, and I don't seem to be quite over it. Can I go back to San?'

I was terrified that Miss Tennyson would work out what Daisy had been doing, but she only put a hand over her eyes.

'Whatever you like,' she said wearily. 'Hazel, take her. Just go to San, both of you.'

7

We did not go to San.

'Why did you do that?' I whispered to Daisy once we were safely out in the corridor. 'What if she *is* the murderer, and she realizes that we're on to her?'

'How on earth would me writhing about on the floor with a piece of string make Miss Tennyson realize that we're on to her?' Daisy whispered back scornfully. 'Don't be silly, Hazel. You're always worrying.'

I didn't think that was fair at all. I was perfectly right to worry. We were on the trail of a killer. How could Daisy be sure that we were safe?

'Anyway,' she went on, 'Miss Tennyson's given us the most perfect opportunity. This is our chance to do some detecting without her around.'

'What sort of detecting?' I asked. It sounded as though Daisy had dreamed up another one of her ideas, and after the ipecac I was beginning to be suspicious of those.

'Can't talk here,' said Daisy. 'Come on – cloakroom.'

Once we got there, though, Daisy did not seem very eager to tell me the details of her new plan. She lay down on one of the benches and pulled the coats down around her, until she was buried under them with only her feet waving about outside.

I sat down next to her. 'Are you all right?' I asked.

'Hazel,' said Daisy from under the coats, 'I know I shouldn't, but I can't help feeling a bit overwhelmed. After all, we're about to catch a *murderer*. That's quite serious, isn't it?'

I kept silent. I was already too worried to feel over-whelmed as well. After a moment the coats rose up in a mountain and Daisy's head burst through them to stare at me accusingly. 'You still don't believe that it's Miss Tennyson, do you?' she asked.

'No,' I said. Despite the evidence of the shoe, I simply could not imagine Miss Tennyson actually pushing Miss Bell over the Gym balcony, no matter how much she might want the Deputy Head job. 'There are so many other possible solutions! What about The One and Miss Parker's row? What about Miss Hopkins sneaking back down to school? And what about Miss Parker? She lied about her alibi and she's been acting ragey all week. What if she lied because she argued with Miss Bell and then killed her? Miss Tennyson fits the facts, but so do three other people! We can't be sure!'

Daisy sighed. 'I didn't think you'd be so jealous about this,' she said. 'Just because I worked it out before you did, and I'm the President and you're only the Secretary. Honestly, Hazel.'

'No!' I cried. 'This is important, Daisy. We can't make a mistake.'

'Look, Hazel,' she said, standing up. 'I'll give you more proof, if you like. When Miss Tennyson moved Miss Bell's body out of Deepdean on Tuesday evening, she must have used that ugly little rattletrap motor car of hers. I'll bet you there's still evidence in it. That's what I want to investigate while we know that Tennyson's stuck in Prep. Oh, come on! Why won't you get up?'

I was still sitting there because I was suddenly stingingly furious at Daisy. I know I've said that there is no point being angry at her, and there is not, but I resented what she had said about her being the President, and me being only the Secretary. After all, there was no reason why Daisy should be a better detective than me. We were looking at the same clues, weren't we? Daisy liked rushing headlong into things and triumphing, and I liked waiting and thinking – but why should that make her right and me wrong?

But Daisy was staring at me appealingly, her big blue eyes wide, and so I clenched my teeth, stood up with a jerk and went to inspect Miss Tennyson's blasted automobile.

It was parked beside the North Entrance gate, a little blue car all scratched and peeling paint, and quite covered in dirt.

'She really does look after it disgustingly,' Daisy commented. 'Just look at that crankcase. I know they're dreadful on these old Sevens, but still!'

'Daisy,' I said, 'how—'

'My uncle,' said Daisy briefly, as though that explained it. She went up to the car and peered inside. I climbed up on the running board to stand beside her.

'If anyone asks us,' said Daisy without looking at me, 'we're looking for our exercise books. Miss Tennyson thought she might have left them here so she sent us down to see.'

I stared into Miss Tennyson's car. It was very like Miss Tennyson, I thought – odd and shabby and rather tragic. I didn't know what Daisy was looking for. As I said, I don't know much about cars – and even less about the inside of Daisy's mind.

Daisy had pulled a hairpin out of her plait and was fiddling with the door handle. Suddenly she said, 'Aha!' thumped the handle and pulled the door open. I wondered how on earth we would explain ourselves if one of the mistresses noticed what we were up to, but Daisy was already burrowing inside. She wriggled almost her entire body into Miss Tennyson's car and her legs, poking out from the bottom of her pinafore, waved around in the air as she searched.

'Hazel, do come here,' she hissed in excitement. I was reluctant. The car seemed very full of Daisy. But when I finally stuck my head in after her, she rolled over and gestured triumphantly at something on the back seat.

It was a stain on the leather as large as my face. It looked as though someone had tried to clean it – the leather was all scratched up and whitish around it – but the stain had soaked in.

'That,' said Daisy to me smugly, 'is blood.'

'It might be anything,' I protested, though I knew that she was right. It looked dark and rusty, exactly like the stains I had found on that gym slip. 'It might be from anything. Perhaps she cut her hand six months ago, Daisy! We can't be sure.'

Daisy snorted. 'Lord!' she said. 'You're difficult. All right, then, I'll find *more* evidence.'

She withdrew from the depths of the car so quickly that she trod on my foot. Then she leaped down from the running board, and began to scrutinize the wheels and front bumper. She sidled crabwise around it, peering intently at every little bit of mud, and I watched her sourly, thinking that the mud looked very much like mud to me.

It obviously meant something more to Daisy. Halfway

round the front left wheel, she gave a little shriek of excitement. 'Look!' she cried. 'Look what's stuck in this spoke!'

I looked. 'It's a leaf,' I said.

'It's not a *leaf*, Hazel,' said Daisy. 'Honestly, didn't you ever *see* the countryside before you came to England? It's lichen, you silly, and I know exactly where it's from. It's that funny orange stuff that only grows at the edge of Oakeshott Woods.'

'Only?' I asked. It still seemed to me that lichen was lichen.

'The only place for fifty miles at least,' said Daisy. 'The only place where Miss Tennyson might go. Whenever I go on hunts there, it gets all over my boots. Now, this stuff isn't new, but it hasn't been here long. I'd say two or three days – taking us back to Tuesday night. Oh, Hazel, what luck! Now we know where she's hidden Miss Bell's body! We've got enough to accuse Miss Tennyson now.'

'But what if she drove over there on Tuesday or Wednesday to go for a walk?' I protested.

'Of course she didn't!' exclaimed Daisy in exasperation. 'We know that after school on Tuesday and Wednesday she was helping Miss Griffin! She wouldn't have been able to go out on her own before it got dark – and who goes for a walk after dark, unless they're doing something nefarious? Look, the only thing we can possibly do now is accuse her. We've really and truly solved the murder!'

She was more excited than I had seen her in a long time. I knew that I ought to feel excited too, but I only felt sick to my stomach. To me, the evidence still did not seem conclusive. There were so many other explanations for everything we had found! I said gruffly, 'Come on, let's go up to House before we get caught.'

'Oh Hazel,' said Daisy, throwing her arms round me. Evidently she had forgotten all about our argument. 'Isn't everything wonderful?'

I wanted to tell her that I did not think things were wonderful at all.

PART SIX

DAISY MAKES HER CASE

1

All the way up to House, Daisy kept going on at me
about her new plan to confront Miss Tennyson, until I
could barely stand it any more.

'We ought to do it soon,' she said. 'After all, we've
got all the evidence we need. It seems quite wrong to
let her off for any longer. If only we could get into her
boarding house and surprise her that way.'

'Isn't that illegal?' I asked. I knew what my father
would say if he heard that I'd been caught breaking into
someone else's property.

'I suppose so,' said Daisy, sighing. 'Isn't it tiresome
being a child? No one lets you do anything. I absolutely *long* to be twenty. I could befriend Miss Tennyson
and lure her into a false sense of security, and then, in
private, and when she was least expecting it, I'd spring
the shoe print and the blood and the moss on her, and
force her to confess.'

'Perhaps it's a good thing you're not twenty,' I said. 'What if you did accuse her, in private, and she killed you too?'

'Goodness,' said Daisy. 'Perhaps a public confrontation would be better. Yes, excellent work, Hazel!' She seized hold of my arm so hard that I had a red mark afterwards. '*That's* the right way to do it. And we can, if we're careful. Today's Saturday, after all.'

Saturday afternoon, you see, is when all the girls are allowed to escape House into Deepdean town for a few hours. There is an order to it, of course. Only prefects are allowed out for the whole afternoon. Matron leads the littlest shrimps in a crocodile, for an hour's outing straight after lunch, on a nice reliable Saturday round of Debenham & Freebody's, the stationer's, the sweetshop and then back to House again. The rest of us are allowed out in pairs, for two-hour chunks. As third form, we go from three till five – enough time for the cinema if you're smart about it; or the sweetshop, the bookshop and then a Lyons' Corner House for tea and cakes, if you're Daisy and me. I was hoping that Daisy's plan, whatever it was, would still leave time for tea and cakes. I was dreading the confrontation with Miss Tennyson, and the thought of undertaking it hungry was even worse.

At lunch time Daisy held a royal audience with her shrimps. As well as Betsy North, she has a trio of identical second formers who are loyal to her. Their names are Marie, Maria and Marion, but we all call them the Marys. They run about in a giddy pack, and seem to add up to one complete person. They have a sort of collective pash on Daisy, and think everything she does is marvellous. She gets the most gorgeous boxes of chocolates from them, and awfully soppy cards which she pretends to appreciate for the sake of the chocolates. When she told them she wanted their help, they nearly went into a collective faint.

'You see,' Daisy told them, 'I've got a sort of bet going with Kitty – you know Kitty, of course.' (The Marys did. Once, last year, Kitty had told one of them to Scram! in the presence of Daisy. The slight had never been forgotten. Daisy knew this perfectly well.) 'Well, Kitty and I were talking about old Tennyson' – the Marys drew in a breath, delighted by this disrespect – 'and that ugly old flat hat she always wears out. I said that it'd be an absolute gift to the world if someone took it off her, and if no one else volunteered, then I'd do the deed myself. Kitty said that I'd never dare, of course, and now I mean to prove her wrong.'

The Marys went pink with shock and excitement. 'Now,' said Daisy, 'you mustn't tell anyone else about this, but when you go out this afternoon I want you to find Miss Tennyson and watch her wherever she goes. Report in to me when you get back to House. And,' she added as an afterthought, 'if you do *especially* well I'll let you carry my book bag about on Monday.'

The Marys almost swooned.

'You can't have them *all* carrying your things,' I said to her afterwards.

'Yes I can,' said Daisy, leaning her head on her arm and staring dreamily at the gluey remains of her shepherd's pie. 'They can each carry a book and someone can take my coat and hat.'

'That's not what I meant,' I said crossly, reaching out with my fork and scooping up the rest of Daisy's pie. I always feel rather bad for Daisy's shrimps. She does use them so, and all because she happens to be beautiful.

It really is unfair, Daisy's beauty. I don't think I've ever seen her with a spot, while all the rest of us are simply covered in them. I have had one particular one on the side of my nose for weeks and weeks. It sits there and refuses to go away. I look at it in the mirror sometimes and want to weep. Meanwhile, Daisy glows, not too pink and not too pale, flawless as a girl in a painting.

I try not to believe the Daisy Wells myth, since I know how much of it is simply nonsense, but I also know that it would not take much for me to end up as silly as the Marys.

2

After lunch, while I was writing up my case notes on our midnight adventure and Daisy's deductions, the first formers filed away obediently behind Matron for their hour's shopping. An hour after that, the Marys waved to Daisy as they trotted off on their own shopping trip, and Daisy waved back like the Queen.

Even though she had sent her minions off to work, Daisy was twitchy. 'What if Miss Tennyson decides to run away?' she asked, pacing up and down the common room with a little crease appearing at the bridge of her nose. 'What if she bolts in her car?'

'She won't,' I said automatically, although really she might very well have done. She would have had the whole afternoon to get clear away. She might be missed on Saturday evening, if there was a curfew at her ladies' boarding house, and she would certainly be missed at Sunday chapel, but she would have a start of hours and hours. Whenever girls run away they do it Saturdays, because of that head start. One Saturday last year Lavinia ran away; she had been missing for six hours before they found her on a bus to Rugby. It was nearly a record.

I suppose, though, that the idea of running did not occur to Miss Tennyson: the Marys came back giddy with pride at having sighted her going into the Willow Tea Rooms.

We were lucky it was November. When we leave school grounds we are supposed to wear our uniforms, but of course it is no good trying to go anywhere grown-up wearing your pinafore and school tie, and the Willow is certainly grown-up. In summer you have to put on your mufti, then your school clothes over the top (breathing in so Matron doesn't notice the difference), and as soon as you're out of school, wriggle out of your uniform. In winter, though, you can get away with just wearing your school coat and hat out of House and bundling them into a bush as soon as you're out of sight down the hill. Of course, once you've done that, you have to grit your teeth and freeze in your pullover, unless you have one of those ultra-fashionable lightweight silk mackintoshes. That day, Daisy wore her mac. I froze.

We walked down the steep hill, slipping a bit on gummy old leaves, past pairs of second formers still straggling back up to House and a bundled-up old lady with a bundly little dog. If it weren't for Miss Bell's murder, I suddenly realized, Daisy and I might still be watching people like that lady, making little case notes about her height and hair colour and suspicious actions. It all seemed rather silly now.

The day was already beginning to fade away and the electric lights illuminated the shop windows of Deepdean Town as we crept into the most overgrown bit of the park. We shook out our plaits, pinned our hair up under our hats (Daisy has the most beautiful berry-coloured cloche that I covet painfully), and shoved our school coats and hats into the middle of a rhododendron bush. I felt awfully regretful as I did it. It is all very well deciding that you are going to sacrifice warmth for the good of detection, but taking off your coat outside in November is not amusing.

Without our uniforms, and with our hair up like grown-ups', there was no way to tell we were Deepdean girls, but we still had to be careful in case we came across a master or mistress.

Daisy was in high spirits. 'I've been working things out in my head,' she said to me as we walked along arm in arm, 'and it's quite clear now. The motive, of course, was the Deputy position. Tennyson wanted it, and thought that if she got Miss Bell out of the way, Miss Griffin'd give it to her instead.

'So Miss Tennyson lured the Bell onto the Gym

balcony on Monday evening and shoved her over the side. She might have still been up on the balcony, but more probably she was down checking on the body when she heard you coming in, so she hid as quick as she could. She knew you'd run for help, so once you'd gone, she dragged Miss Bell's body into the Cupboard before you came back with me and Virginia. She waited, and when the coast was clear she ran for Jones's spare keys – or she might have got hold of them earlier in the day, I suppose – loaded Miss Bell onto the trolley from the Gym cupboard, and pushed her down to the tunnel. She faked that resignation note from Miss Bell and left it on Miss Griffin's desk on Tuesday morning, then crept back at night to take the body right out of the school. She smashed the New Wing corridor window on the way, of course – she *is* terribly clumsy – then put the body in her car, and drove it out to the woods to hide it for good.'

A series of vivid images went dancing through my mind. I saw Miss Tennyson – who was afraid of creepy crawly creatures, and very afraid of the dark – dragging Miss Bell's body into the storeroom, and wheeling it down into the dark tunnel on her own. It simply did not seem possible. But what if Daisy was right?

Daisy was still talking.

'You know, if her conscience hadn't begun to play up, we might never have properly suspected her, not when Miss Parker seemed so promising. Really, Miss Tennyson managed a rather neat murder. She didn't make the mistake of trying to be too clever. It's always the clever ones who get found out easy as anything. My uncle says so.'

When Daisy laid it out like that, it all seemed to make sense. I wondered if I were really just jealous of Daisy. Was I being a bad member of the Detective Society in not agreeing with the President? I was very confused.

Just then we reached the Willow Tea Rooms. Unlike Lyons, the teashop where Daisy and I usually go, which has waxy potted palms and stacks of brightly iced cakes displayed behind its enormous glass shopfront, the Willow has little windowpanes shyly half covered with chintz curtains and a blue front door with a tinkling bell. It is a polite place, all draped in cloth, and the dainty little sugared cakes which arrive on matching blue-and-white patterned plates are so small that you can hardly get a proper bite of them.

I paused on the doorstep. Even after being friends with Daisy for nearly a year, I still feel a guilty lurch in my stomach whenever we go somewhere we're not allowed. Daisy, though, was cool as a cucumber about it. Things like that don't worry her at all. She walked in as though she was going into the Dining Room at House.

Miss Tennyson was sitting alone at a table near the door, her thick-waisted out-of-fashion tweed coat on her lap and her ugly old flat-brimmed wool hat crumpled up next to her plate. The chair next to her was empty. When we came in, she started and half turned round on her seat. Her eyes flicked over us, but I could tell that she wasn't really seeing us at all.

Daisy, very chic in her cloche hat and lipstick – which Kitty had swapped her for a diamond pin that looked very nearly real – managed to get us the table next to Miss Tennyson and order tea and a plate of sugar cakes. She was speaking loudly, but Miss Tennyson was so wrapped up in whatever her thoughts that she still did not notice us. I think Daisy was a bit cross about that. She made a great clattering of her spoon against her saucer, dropped her hat at Miss Tennyson's feet, and at last cleared her throat, turned round on her chair and said, 'Miss Tennyson!'

Miss Tennyson jumped as though someone had shot her.

3

Miss Tennyson's eyes flicked over Daisy's face and she spoke in a small creaky voice that was quite unlike her usual one. 'Daisy! What are you doing here?'

'I've come to see you,' said Daisy meaningfully.

'Whatever for?' asked Miss Tennyson. 'Daisy, this is not a place for children. Does Matron know you're here?'

Then she caught sight of me for the first time. 'Hazel,' she said blankly. 'What is this?'

'We're here,' said Daisy, pausing to enjoy the moment, 'because *we know what you've done.*'

Miss Tennyson's large bony hands, pressing tightly down on the flowery tablecloth, twitched. Then she clenched them together so hard her knuckles turned white. I could see the bones right through her skin. 'Daisy,' Miss Tennyson whispered, 'whatever do you mean?'

'We know!' said Daisy, speaking very quickly. 'We

know you killed Miss Bell! We've seen the blood on the Gym cupboard trolley, and your footprints in the tunnel, and the blood in your car, and then there's *this* . . .' And she stuck out her hand and seized Miss Tennyson's left arm in its shapeless knitted pullover.

Miss Tennyson yelped in pain, so that the waitress turned and stared at our table curiously. The arm Daisy had taken hold of showed the faint lines of a bandage tied under Miss Tennyson's pullover. *No!* I thought. *Oh no!*

'The evidence against you is damning,' continued Daisy. (I thought she might be drawing on her murder mysteries a little too heavily.) 'And I haven't even shown you the best bit – I mean, the most important piece of evidence – yet. Look!' She put her hand in her pocket, drew out the earring and brandished it in front of Miss Tennyson's trembling face.

Miss Tennyson burst into tears. She put her face in her hands and sobbed and sobbed and sobbed. My heart sank. I really had hoped that she would deny everything, but as a sign of guilt, this was unmistakable. I had to believe Daisy now.

Through the sobbing, Miss Tennyson was trying to say something. 'Sorry,' we heard. 'So sorry – I wish—'

'At least she isn't denying it,' whispered Daisy to me over our willow-patterned plate of cakes. 'I think this is going rather well, don't you?'

I did not.

At last, Miss Tennyson sat up in her seat and stared at us both. She was looking extremely unlike a mistress by then. Her eyes were swollen and red, and her nose was red as well. I knew Daisy was thinking what an absolute fright she looked.

'It's utter hell,' Miss Tennyson said quietly. 'I've been in hell. The last few days – it's all been a blur. I can't think any more. How did you find out? No, no, don't tell me. I can't bear any more. I'm just so bloody *tired*.'

It was the first time I had ever heard a mistress swear. It's silly, but until then I had simply assumed that they must not know how to. Miss Tennyson saying *bloody* gave me the most dreadful shock.

Daisy, of course, was thinking more practically. 'You must give yourself up,' she told Miss Tennyson sternly. 'To the police, immediately. If you don't go, we will.'

Miss Tennyson was squeezing and squeezing that old hat of hers, as though she was trying to crush the life out of it, but her face had gone very calm. 'I shall,' she said. 'There's nothing else to be done, is there? It's funny – I've read so much about guilt, and I always thought I understood it, but this – I can't bear it any more, it's as simple as that. Confessing is the only way to—' Suddenly the peaceful look fell off her face and she looked terrified again. 'But girls – you mustn't be mixed up in all this. Don't tell anyone you were here. If

I go to the police, they won't need your evidence; you won't be dragged into it. Do you promise?'

'Yes,' I said. 'I promise.' Then I looked at Daisy. She was obviously in the grip of a terrible personal struggle.

'I promise,' she said at last, rather sulkily. 'But if you don't go—'

'I will!' said Miss Tennyson sharply. 'I will. Now leave, girls.'

'We shall,' said Daisy. 'And *you* may pay our bill, *if* you please.'

It was an utterly Daisy exit to make. In any other circumstances I would have laughed, but something was niggling away at me. Why had Miss Tennyson been so desperate for us to leave? Was it simply that she did not want us getting mixed up with the police, as she had said? Or – I remembered how she had jumped round in her chair as we had come in – had she been *waiting* for someone? Was she meeting someone in the Willow that she did not want us to know about?

'Daisy,' I said, turning to look at her as we stepped through the door outside, making the little bell chime as we did so, 'do you think—'

And then the rest of the sentence was knocked right out of me as I thumped straight into someone coming the other way down the street. I yelped and the other person exclaimed in annoyance. Then I gave a gasp of surprise. I was staring up at the chestnut curls and regal nose of King Henry.

As soon as she saw us, she spun on her heel and marched away up the street again – but I was sure that she had been about to go into the Willow. What if – what if she was the person Miss Tennyson had been waiting for? And if she was, that meant that there was more to this mystery than Daisy's solution. I had been right all along.

'Daisy!' I said. 'I think King Henry was about to go into the Willow!'

'So?' asked Daisy.

'*So*, I think she was going to meet Miss Tennyson! Daisy, I think she's mixed up in this somehow. There's something going on that we don't understand yet!'

'No there isn't,' snapped Daisy. 'Don't be stupid, Hazel! We've solved the murder and that's that. Leave off, can't you?'

'No, I can't,' I said. 'We *haven't* solved the murder. King Henry as good as proves it. I tell you—'

'Oh, DO BE QUIET!' shouted Daisy. 'I don't want to hear another word about it. I'm thinking, can't you see?'

All I could see was that Daisy knew she had been wrong, and was being a terribly bad sport about it.

'All right,' I said, 'be like that.' And I stormed back up to House without saying another word to her.

4

Things were still cold between us when we arrived back at House. We were greeted by the Marys, who mobbed Daisy to ask if they had helped.

'Wonderfully,' said Daisy acidly. 'Although the hat remained elusive. You may carry my coat if you like.' She flung her school coat and hat at the Marys, who bore them off to the cloakroom in raptures. I do not think they knew what *elusive* meant.

We were not talking, and for a while I was glad about it. I decided that I was not going to speak to Daisy until she admitted that I had been right all along. When Kitty, Beanie and Lavinia came back from town, they asked Daisy to make up a fourth for cribbage and I was left sitting alone in an armchair in the common room, writing up my case notes and thinking about Daisy and me. It is difficult being best friends with someone, especially if that someone is Daisy Wells. She hates being wrong. It is infuriating. But every time I want to simply give up being the sensible one, and shake her, I remember that before Daisy and I became friends I was even worse off.

You see, as I've already suggested, my time at Deepdean did not begin well. When I first came here I raised my hand every time I knew an answer, just the way my father had taught me. In return, though, I got cold little looks from the other girls, who inched their chairs away from me, as though I had an illness that might be catching. Girls who were meant to walk back to House with me would duck away and go running to where their friends were waiting, and when I sat down at the table for dinner, everyone pulled their trays back very slightly and bent their heads together, looking at me from out of the corner of their eyes.

I thought I had to grin and bear it, but that was before I understood about the secret side of Daisy. When I did, though, I realized that if the great Daisy Wells could play a role, I could play one too. I could behave like a don't-care girl on the outside, but inside I could still be me. The important thing about fitting in, I realized, was to *look* the part. And so I decided to do just that.

Some things, of course, were beyond me. When I let it out of its plait, my hair will always fall straight down to my shoulders without any fetching natural waves in it at all, and my eyes will always be brown, instead of large and blue. So I saw that I would have to go about camouflaging myself another way.

In a quiet moment in the dorm one day, when most of the second form were at hockey practice and the rest were in the common room, I filched Lavinia's penknife from her tuck box and made a careful cut in one of my shoelaces. I tugged it and wiggled it about until the end snapped off entirely, leaving behind a satisfyingly authentic-looking frayed shoelace. Then, offering up a silent apology to my father for what I was about to do, I picked up my hockey stick, gripped it in both hands and whacked it as hard as I could against the side of my school bag. It hit home with a surprisingly heavy *smack* and the books inside of the bag thumped about against each other under the canvas. I had the uncomfortable feeling I had just hit something that was alive. I managed one more *thwack* before I completely lost heart, but that was good enough – my books were now bent about as though I had been mistreating them for months. I felt dreadfully guilty about the books, but I told myself firmly that it was worth it.

The next morning, after Kitty and Lavinia ran off as usual and left me alone, I was careful to walk down to school very slowly, scuffing my clean, shiny shoes along the dirty path with every step and then knocking the mud against the outside of my bag. By the time I arrived late at Old Wing Entrance I was left with a perfectly weathered-looking bag and a pair of shoes that were more mud than polish.

At bunbreak I sat on the low wall next to the lawn and worked on my shoes a little more by kicking them against the crumbling stonework. This gave them some very artistic scratches, which I was rather pleased with. I rubbed my fingernails across them, smearing my fingers about to catch all the dirt I could, and then held my hands up in front of me. They might, I thought, looking at the grime round my cuticles, almost be the hands of an English girl.

My plan was going very well so far, and after lunch I decided to proceed with the next stage. Until then I had answered every question as soon as I knew it, but now I resolved to take a leaf out of Daisy's book. In Maths, I added up a sum wrong three times in a row, and in my French composition I told Mamzelle that I had brown eyes and a long black horse.

When I read this out, I got my first ever giggle from the second form, and after lessons Lavinia walked all the way back up to House with me – silently, but without leaving me behind at all. The next day I found the book I had asked Kitty if I could borrow weeks before lying on my bed, and at bunbreak, after I had confused my tenses four times in Latin, Beanie sympathetically gave me some of the spare Chelsea bun she had found lying on the floor.

Two days in to my new act, I was feeling very smug with myself. In Science, I wiggled down in my seat and tried to look as don't-care as possible – copying Lavinia, who was hunched over with her arms crossed and her feet curled round her chair legs in a way that, according to Miss Lappet, was extremely dangerous and could lead to broken limbs or worse. When Miss Bell came in I began to sit up straight before I remembered I mustn't. To make up for it, I dropped a Bunsen burner and then said that Newton shot an apple at his son, which made Beanie squeal with laughter.

'Whatever has happened to you today, Hazel?' asked Miss Bell, raising an eyebrow. 'I think you've been spending too much time around Beanie.'

Beanie flushed deep red and looked down hurriedly at her textbook, and most of the second form glared at Miss Bell.

There was one person, though, not looking at Miss Bell – when I glanced over at Daisy, I saw that her blue eyes were fixed on me, in an all-over searching way that made me turn almost as pink as Beanie and look down again as quickly as I could. I carefully spent the rest of the lesson fixing my eyes on everything but Daisy's bench, and answered no more questions at all.

As punishment for the Bunsen burner, Miss Bell made me tidy the lab at the end of our lesson. By the time I was finished I thought everyone would have hurried away to Latin, but the door banged to behind me and when I turned round, there was Daisy, leaning against a bench and waiting for me.

I tried to walk past her.

'Stop there,' said Daisy, and she stuck her foot out in front of me. She had mud on her sock. 'What do you think you're doing?'

'I'm going to Latin,' I said, rather weakly.

'Not what I meant,' said Daisy. 'Look at your shoes. Until two days ago you might have been in the military, and now it looks as though you've been rolling in mud.'

'I fell over,' I said, more weakly still.

All of a sudden, Daisy launched herself off her bench and crouched down at my feet. Her breath made my ankle itch, and I wriggled. 'You've cut this shoelace,' she declared after a moment, squinting up at me accusingly. 'And all the scratches on your shoes are new as well. Before this week I'd never seen you with a button out of place. I was beginning to think they hadn't heard of dirt in the East. So, what are you playing at?'

That upset me. 'I'm fitting in!' I snapped. 'Just like you do!'

Daisy bobbed up again. She was taller than me, and she looked down on me ferociously. I backed away, thinking she was about to do something awful.

'Whatever do you mean?' she asked.

'I've seen you!' I said. 'You pretend not to know the answer when I *know* you do, all the time, just to make sure no one calls you a swot. Really, you're cleverer than any of us. I've been watching you and I know it's true. And if you tell anyone that I cut off my own lace I'll tell everyone about *you*.'

I expected Daisy to be furious. Instead, she laughed.

'I doubt anyone would listen to you,' she said. '*You* ought to be more careful, by the way. You're making a dreadful job of it. You can't just launch into this sort of thing with no warning. People don't change character like that outside of silly made-up stories. If you're going to do it, you need to be more subtle about it. You don't want people to look at you unless you're very good at acting.'

'But people look at you!' I said.

'I,' said Daisy, '*am* very good at acting. But you mustn't tell anyone or I shall have to have you killed. Now hurry up, or we'll be late for Latin.' And with that she put out her hand, hooked her arm through mine and dragged me out of the laboratory.

And that was how Daisy Wells and I became best friends.

PART SEVEN

WE RUN INTO TROUBLE

1

Daisy and I are still not talking, and I have been wondering whether this case will be the Detective Society's last. Seeing King Henry yesterday made me certain that justice has not yet been done, and now I feel sure that something has gone very wrong with Miss Tennyson's confession. I am worried.

Today is Sunday, and this morning we woke up to find the day as grim and grey as I have been feeling. We all filed off to Sunday service in the Hall under spattering dark clouds. Everyone cringed and scurried, and Daisy and Kitty darted between the drops together, arm in arm. Evidently, Daisy did not mind that she and I were not speaking.

Miss Tennyson was not at Sunday service.

That was not odd. If she had gone to the police after we left her yesterday, she would still be there now – arrested, in her cell, and waiting for the trial, I suppose.

Or for the police to find Miss Bell's body. (When I try to imagine what happens after someone confesses to murder, I can't seem to do it properly – I suppose because Daisy's books are so coy about it.)

But the really worrying thing was that the rest of the masters and mistresses were still behaving perfectly normally. It was as though they had not heard about Miss Tennyson confessing to a murder. Miss Hopkins, for example, was still wearing her smug, happy expression, while Miss Parker was still sizzling with bottled-up rage.

Mr MacLean's Sunday sermon was exactly as dull as it usually is, all about friendship (I thought of Daisy, bitterly), good works and the importance of beautifying the world. I listened to it and felt as though I had come into the wrong sermon by mistake and if I looked at the date I would see that it was five weeks ago, or years and years in the future.

The One began to play the hymn, and as she stood up Miss Lappet swayed.

'Drunk again,' whispered Kitty to Daisy, loud enough for me to overhear. 'Hasn't she been bad this week? Rumour has it that she's in mourning for the Deputy job. I heard from one of the Big Girls that she went to confront Miss Griffin about it on Monday evening. They had an appointment straight after socs, and Miss Griffin finally told her that she hadn't a hope. Miss Lappet ran straight out of Miss Griffin's office, apparently, and has been on the demon drink ever since.'

'What?' I said, much too loudly. My heart had suddenly started pounding so hard that I could feel it through my pinafore.

'*Seeeng*, girls!' snapped Mamzelle, without turning round.

I could not believe what I had just heard. Miss Lappet had only been in Miss Griffin's office for a few minutes. Her alibi had been wiped out, just like that, and now there was nothing to say that Miss Lappet had not been in the Gym at the crucial time, pushing Miss Bell off the balcony.

I slid a look at Daisy out of the corner of my eye and saw that she was very determinedly not looking back at me. But there was a worry-line creasing the top of her nose, and I could tell – just as certainly as if she had said it – that Daisy had finally realized just how wrong she was.

After the service we walked back up to House behind Matron, two by two. I was next to Lavinia – who was being her usual lumpish, moody self – and all at once I decided that I could not bear arguing with Daisy any longer. We had to solve the mystery together. As soon as we were back up at House, and safe in the noise of the common room, I ran up and seized her arm. 'Daisy!' I cried. 'I'm sorry, I've been behaving like a beast.'

Daisy turned to look at me with a strange expression on her face. I could not make it out. 'Hazel,' she said after a moment, 'I refuse your apology.'

I gaped at her.

'Because,' Daisy continued, lifting her chin proudly, '*I* was wrong, and so it should be me apologizing.'

'But, Daisy—'

'Hazel, will you let me talk? Whether or not Miss Tennyson did it, there are too many things going on that don't fit my theory. You knew that, and you told me so, and you were right.'

'I was thinking . . .' I said, bracing myself for Daisy to ignore me again. 'What if someone did the murder *with* Miss Tennyson? She and Miss Lappet, or – or she and Miss Parker. And King Henry's got to be involved *somehow*, I know it!'

To my surprise, Daisy nodded. 'It's possible,' she said. 'Oh, Hazel, I've been a terrible Detective Society President. I ought to have listened to you instead of rushing about like a fool. Why haven't we heard about Miss Tennyson going to the police yet?'

'I don't know,' I said, beginning to worry all over again. 'Do you think she's done a bunk?'

Daisy made a face. 'I hope she's done a bunk,' she said, 'because all the alternatives I can imagine are even worse.'

*

We spent the rest of the day swapping theories, and although most of them were utterly silly, it was wonderful to have Daisy finally listening to me for a change.

'Perhaps Miss Tennyson's in love with The One too,' I said. 'And she found out he'd done it, and helped him cover up the crime.'

'Or perhaps she's The One's long-lost sister!' said Daisy. It was after dinner, and she was sprawled on her bed with one foot, in its regulation white sock, waving in the air. I stared down at her. 'All right, all right, I was only joking. What I mean to say is, perhaps King Henry is Miss Tennyson's long-lost daughter. Ow! No need to hit me like that!'

'You aren't being serious,' I told her.

'Well, neither are you,' said Daisy. 'It'd be far more productive for you to do some secretarying and write up what's happened today.'

So I did. Going over it like this has made me worried all over again. If Miss Tennyson didn't go to the police – which seems more and more likely, since none of us have heard about it – *why* didn't she? Has she simply done a runner, or has something else happened to her?

I am trying not to think about what that something else could be.

2

We know now that Miss Tennyson has not run away.

On Monday morning Daisy and I walked down to school together, friends again, to discover that things had gone badly wrong at Deepdean.

The first sign came at registration: on Mondays it is usually Miss Tennyson who takes our register, but today Mamzelle rushed in two minutes late, looking flustered, and read off our names at such a terrific pace she forgot to roll her Rs. I felt sick with worry.

We filed out of the room for Prayers, Mamzelle pursing her lips in alarm and shooing us along with her hands flapping, and made it into the Hall just as The One gave the organ its last few warning blares. When we passed Miss Lappet on the way to our seats I could smell the drink wafting off her.

Miss Griffin made her entrance while we were still shuffling along our row, and she stood and waited for us, glaring sternly down over the lectern.

At last, when we were settled and there was nothing to be heard but our breathing, Miss Griffin cleared her throat. She leaned her hands against the lectern and stared down at us, and then she began to speak. Miss Griffin's morning lectures are like Miss Griffin herself – clean and rigorous and slightly frightening. They always make me feel sinkingly inadequate, as though I'm being spoken to by the voice of God. I know I will never be as good as Miss Griffin assumes we all are. She is so terribly good herself that she puts the rest of us to shame.

At the end of the lecture came the weekly match scores (Firsts hockey against St Chator's, 7-8; Seconds netball against Dee Hill 24-18), and then the general announcements – the Drama Soc was performing *King Lear*, donations were being taken for the RSPCA. Then a pause. We all looked up. Miss Griffin's serene forehead was creased. 'And I am sorry to have to announce, girls, that over the weekend Miss Tennyson suffered a terrible accident. She was taken to hospital, but unfortunately there was nothing to be done. Girls, I am so sorry. Miss Tennyson is no longer with us.'

There was a frozen silence, and then everyone began to talk at once. Miss Griffin opened her mouth, closed it again with a wince, signalled to The One at the organ and marched off the stage. The One dropped his hands onto the keys with a smash and everyone had to shriek at each other to be heard through the din. A few of the shrimps were crying.

I cannot have been thinking straight, because it took me a moment to realize what Miss Griffin really meant. *No longer with us* was just a very nice way of saying *dead*. And as soon as I realized that, I felt cold all over. Was it really true? An accident? It seemed simply too convenient. What if – my heart sank – Miss Tennyson had not been able to face lying in her confession to the police (for by now I was quite sure that she would have been lying, although I had no idea why), and had taken another way out? People did it in books all the time, heroically and beautifully, and I knew that Miss Tennyson believed in books.

Daisy seized my arm. Her eyes were glittering.

'How can you look like that?' I asked. 'Miss Tennyson's killed herself – oh, Daisy, I think it's our fault!'

'Killed *herself*?' said Daisy blankly. 'Oh no. She didn't kill herself. And she didn't suffer an accident either. She's been murdered. Just like you thought, someone helped her with Miss Bell's murder, and now her accomplice has killed her.'

'No!' I gasped.

'Yes,' said Daisy. 'It's the only thing that makes sense.'

'But Daisy, even if someone else killed Miss Tennyson,

it's still our fault. If we hadn't told Miss Tennyson to go to the police, then she'd be alive!'

Daisy snorted. 'Well, it'll teach her to go about murdering people,' she said. 'Is it our fault that she helped kill Miss Bell?'

Strictly, of course, she was quite right, but I still felt vilely responsible. Daisy does not understand this sort of thing because it is not logical, but I knew perfectly well that somehow we had caused Miss Tennyson's death.

'But what shall we do?' I asked.

Daisy looked at me as though I was mad. '*Do?*' she asked. 'The only thing we can do. Keep on until we catch Miss Tennyson's accomplice and solve both murders, of course.'

3

We were lucky that our conversation was lost in the roar of noise from the rest of the school. The masters, mistresses and prefects were trying to hush us up and shoo us out of the Hall, but they could not possibly quiet all of us. King Henry was not even trying. She was leaning against the back of a wooden bench, her face pale, and I was more certain than ever that she had something to do with the mystery.

The whole school was in a panic. What had happened at our séance came back into everyone's minds with a vengeance. No matter what Miss Griffin had said about accidents, everyone decided that this was yet another murder.

No one did any work all morning. In French, after struggling with us for ten minutes, Mamzelle threw up her hands, put a French composition on the board, took out *Weldon's Ladies' Journal* and left us to it.

'I can't believe that Miss Tennyson's been murdered too,' said Kitty. 'Just like Miss Bell. Two in two weeks!'

'They're both going to come back and haunt the school,' said Lavinia loudly, to frighten Beanie. 'Just you wait.'

Beanie burst into tears. 'But I liked Miss Tennyson,' she wailed. 'I don't want her to be *murdered*.'

'Girls,' shouted Mamzelle, her French accent back with a vengeance, 'Mees Tennyson 'as *not been murdered*! Please go back to your compositions and let us have no more of zis!' Then she shook back her dyed hair, turned to 'The Fashion in Furs' and ignored us again.

The next lesson was Maths. As we went into the room, I stared at Miss Parker nervously. Was she displaying any new signs of guilt? I couldn't see any, exactly, but her cropped hair was sticking up like a brush so I knew she must be troubled.

She bawled at us to sit down in her most sergeant-major-ish voice, and then we went through maths problems rigorously. None of us could pay attention. We made the most fearful mistakes, and that made Miss Parker bawl at us even harder. At last, just before the end of the lesson, Beanie put her head in her hands and burst into tears – but Miss Parker didn't tell her to be quiet. Indeed, she suddenly looked as though she was about to weep herself.

'Miss Parker,' said Kitty, as Beanie sobbed, 'what happened to Miss Tennyson?'

'I'm sorry, Kitty,' said Miss Parker in a husky voice, 'I don't know.'

I realized that I believed her. Miss Parker, for all her raging, was truly upset about Miss Tennyson's death – and not just upset, but *confused*. She didn't know what had happened any more than we did. And if that was true, it meant that Miss Parker was not the murderer. But how was I going to prove it to Daisy?

I looked over at Daisy. The small crease across the bridge of her nose had appeared again. I knew she was not upset about Miss Tennyson in the same way I was. Guilt slides straight off Daisy like butter; I don't imagine she's ever felt it properly. I could tell that she was planning something.

'Put your things away, girls,' Miss Parker told us, still in the same lost voice. 'You may go to bunbreak early today.'

Immediately, Daisy leaned down to pick up her bag – and straightened up again with a very loud, 'OH!'

Several people jumped. 'What is it, Daisy?' asked Miss Parker.

'I think I've found your earring, Miss Parker,' said Daisy. 'It was lying on the floor, next to my bag. Look!'

Miss Parker barely glanced at it. 'Not mine, Daisy,' she said without interest as she swept our exercise books into a stack. 'Although it looks like one of the ones Mr—' She stopped halfway through her sentence. 'Oh, never mind. Off you go, girls!'

As soon as we were out of the room, Daisy seized my arm. 'She didn't do it!' she said.

'I know!' I said in great relief. 'Thank goodness you proved it, I didn't know how I would. And did you hear what Miss Parker said when you showed her the earring? Something about it looking like "one of the ones *Mr*" – I'll *bet* she meant The One. He's the only Mr at Deepdean who might be giving out earrings.'

Daisy clapped me on the back. 'Watson,' she said, 'your detective talents continue to amaze me. I may end up promoting you.'

I nearly pointed out that since there was no one in the Society but the two of us, it was quite difficult to see how I could be promoted.

'But for now—'

The bell rang for bunbreak. Miss Parker came out of the classroom behind us and hurried away.

'Oh, quick, follow her! She may not be a suspect any more, but I have a hunch that she may still be important!'

4

Daisy and I followed Miss Parker at a breakneck pace, through the struggling, gossiping (and often weeping) crowds of girls thronging the corridors, all the way to The One's cubby. Luckily for us, she did not look back once, not even after she had knocked on his door.

'Come in!' called The One, and Miss Parker practically threw herself inside.

Giving each other deeply significant looks, Daisy and I positioned ourselves one on each side of the steps, leaned as close to the closed cubby door as we could and listened with all our might.

Luckily for us, it wasn't long before both of them began shouting. Miss Parker shouted first.

'This has gone far enough!'

There was a rumble from The One.

'No, I won't have it! This isn't a game any more!

Amelia Tennyson is dead. Dead! Do you blame me for worrying about what's happened to Joan?'

'I certainly blame you for being a BLOODY MADWOMAN,' said The One, loud enough to be heard through the door.

I flinched and gasped. Daisy giggled in excitement.

'Why won't you tell me where she is? You must know!' Miss Parker sounded desperate now.

'Will you GET OUT OF MY OFFICE?' roared The One.

Daisy and I dived away from the door, just as Miss Parker came slamming back out, red-faced and furious.

'GET OUT OF MY WAY!' she shrieked at a group of innocent second formers. She pushed past them blindly and hurried off towards the mistresses' common room.

'Arguing again,' said one of the second formers to her friends, rolling her eyes.

'What do *you* know about it?' asked Daisy.

The second formers looked quite excited to be addressed by such a glamorous third former.

'Miss Parker's cross,' explained the ringleader, Kitty's little sister Binny. 'It's because Miss Hopkins is engaged to The One, and Miss Parker hates them both. *You* know why.'

'They *can't* be engaged!' gasped Daisy. I was thunderstruck. I'd guessed that The One and Miss Hopkins were in league, but I had never thought that things might have gone so far between them.

'Of course she is,' said Binny. 'That's why Miss Hopkins has been so pathetically happy. It happened last Friday. They're keeping it secret so Miss Griffin doesn't fire them. Isn't Miss Hopkins lucky? He's so *dreamy*.'

Daisy's face had gone as red as Miss Parker's.

'You're an infernal liar, Binny Freebody,' she snapped. 'Come on, Hazel, we've got bigger fish to fry.'

'I am NOT!' Binny shrieked at us as we marched away. 'IT'S TRUE! You're just BITTER!'

Of course Binny was quite right. Daisy hates to be outdone on knowledge of Deepdean goings-on. And missing something as important as an engagement! I could tell she was kicking herself about it.

We found a safe space to talk by the pond at the edge of the north lawn. 'I was wrong about Miss Parker blackmailing The One,' I said, to cheer Daisy up. 'All she was asking him to do was tell her where Miss Bell was.'

Daisy nodded. 'When Miss Bell disappeared, Miss Parker thought that The One knew something about it. Of course, *we* know that Miss Bell didn't run away with him, because she was dead, but the fact that Miss Parker doesn't know means that we have to rule her out once and for all.'

'What if Miss Hopkins and The One *did* do it

together?' I asked. 'If Miss Bell discovered their engagement – you know how Miss Griffin hates it when her mistresses get married, she thinks they've betrayed her. She'd have dismissed them both on the spot – so perhaps they killed her to keep it a secret? After all, we've as good as heard Miss Parker say that the earring we found looks like some The One gave to Miss Hopkins – and aren't you supposed to give jewellery to the person you're in love with?'

I said it without thinking, and then winced, remembering that my accusation of Miss Hopkins had caused our argument in the first place. But Miss Tennyson's murder really must have done something to Daisy. She opened her mouth to shout at me, but then she closed it again and frowned thoughtfully.

'No, you're right,' she said at last. 'We can't discount Miss Hopkins any more. I don't want her to have done it, but we must follow the clues wherever they take us. The only question is, why would she and The One rope Miss Tennyson into it? He's got a car, after all, and he's strong enough to help Miss Hopkins move the body.'

'Perhaps they wanted to use her as . . . as a scapegoat,' I suggested. 'So if someone *did* discover there had been a murder, they could blame Miss Tennyson for it. But then they started to worry that she would tell someone the truth, so they decided to get rid of her.'

'And run away to begin their new lives together!'

said Daisy. 'Not bad, Watson. Not bad at all! I'm more and more certain that we're very close. Only a few real suspects left! We need to have a proper Detective Society meeting about it at lunch time, though, just to make sure we're doing everything we ought.'

We gave each other the Detective Society handshake just as the bell rang, and I went off to lessons with the remaining suspects swimming about in my head.

Either Miss Hopkins and The One had done it, or Miss Lappet had.

And we had some new information to add to our suspect list too.

SUSPECT LIST

1. ~~Miss Parker.~~ ~~MOTIVE:~~ ~~Jealous rage.~~
~~ALIBI:~~ ~~None yet between 5.20 and 5.45 p.m.~~
~~NOTES:~~ ~~Was seen arguing with the victim~~
~~at 4.20 on the day of the murder and at 5.20~~
~~seen alone in New Wing form room (near Gym)~~
~~by Kitty Freebody. Believes the victim is still~~
~~alive and her whereabouts are known by The One.~~
RULED OUT.

2. ~~Miss Hopkins~~. ~~MOTIVE:~~ ~~Getting~~
~~rid of a love rival.~~ Miss Bell threatened
to reveal her secret engagement to The One.
~~ALIBI:~~ ~~Good. Up in Pavilion at time of murder.~~
~~RULED OUT~~ None between 5.20 and
5.45. NOTES: May be in league with The
One.

3. Miss Lappet. MOTIVE: Wants the
Deputy Headmistress job. ALIBI: ~~None yet.~~
None between 5.20 and 5.50pm. NOTES:
Was seen going into Miss Griffin's study
just after 4.30, in agitated state, by Felicity
Carrington, then leaving shortly after. Observed to
have been drunk several times since the murder —
guilty conscience?

4. ~~Miss Tennyson~~. ~~MOTIVE:~~ ~~Wants~~
~~the Deputy Headmistress job.~~ ~~ALIBI:~~ ~~None~~
~~yet between 5.20 and 5.50.~~ ~~NOTES:~~ ~~Was~~
~~observed near Gym just after murder by Daisy~~
~~Wells and Hazel Wong.~~ The second victim! But
may have been used by the murderer in some way.

5. *Mamzelle.* ~~MOTIVE: None. ALIBI: None yet. Good. In Music Wing between 5.20 and 5.45, observed by Sophie Croke-Finchley. NOTES: Was seen near to Gym just after murder, by Daisy Wells and Hazel Wong.~~ RULED OUT.

6. *Mr MacLean.* ~~MOTIVE: None. ALIBI: None yet. Good. In study with class of confirmation students between 5.20 and 5.45. NOTES: Was seen near to Gym just after murder, by Daisy Wells and Hazel Wong.~~ RULED OUT.

7. *The One.* MOTIVE: ~~Anger? Blackmail? None yet.~~ Miss Bell threatened to reveal his secret engagement to Miss Hopkins. ALIBI: ~~None yet.~~ Taking Sophie Croke-Finchley for music lesson between 4.20 and 4.50 but none yet between 5.20 and 5.45. NOTES: Was observed near Gym just after murder by Daisy Wells and Hazel Wong. May be in league with Miss Hopkins.

7. *King Henry.* MOTIVE: Unclear. ALIBI: Unclear. NOTES: Probably not the murderer, but she has something to do with this case. What is it?

5

At lunch time, everyone was loudly distraught, even though Miss Tennyson had not been a popular mistress, and had not had a clique of favourites, like Miss Hopkins or Miss Griffin. When Miss Tennyson was alive, most people had thought her rather wet and foolish. But I was beginning to see that as soon as someone is dead, everyone else feels horribly guilty for *not* caring about them and goes wild trying to prove that they did. Everyone was afraid of the murderer too.

'I sent a telegram to Mummy asking her to take me out of school,' I heard one fifth former say to her friends as I passed them. 'At this rate we shall have no mistresses left, and I don't want to be the next victim!'

There were the usual rumours about how Miss Tennyson had died. It had happened in her boarding house, that much was known, so there was a popular theory involving a horrible shove down the stairs. Daisy listened carefully to all the gossip at the House lunch table, and then went off to find out the truth from King Henry. She came back fuming.

'Veronal,' she said briefly. 'Overdose. According to King Henry, Miss Tennyson's doctor prescribed it for her ages ago – she had trouble sleeping. Still, because it's unnatural death it'll have to be investigated. Oh, bother!'

'What's wrong?' I asked, not quite understanding why Daisy was so upset. 'Is it King Henry? Did she say anything important?'

'The police are going to be called in, you chump. Imagine! The police! They'll ruin everything. They won't even interview any of the girls, only the masters and mistresses, because they'll think we're not important!'

'Well, we aren't important,' I said.

Daisy narrowed her eyes and fixed me with an icy blue stare. '*I* am important,' she said. 'I'm the only one who's been investigating this murder from the start – apart from you, I mean, Hazel. Sorry. Well, they'll see! This is our school and no one has any right to go about bumping people off in it.'

'But what if the police solve the murders before we do?' I asked.

'They won't,' said Daisy. 'They don't even know that they're murders, or that there have been two of them!

235

The police just think they're investigating a suicide. But *we* know that Miss Bell and Miss Tennyson were murdered, and we know who the suspects are. Which means that we're still the only people who can solve the crimes.'

I had to admit that Daisy's logic made sense. Under the circumstances, in fact, the Detective Society had never seemed so important.

6

'I declare this extraordinary meeting of the Detective Society to discuss the Case of the Murder of Miss Bell to order,' said Daisy. 'In the light of Miss Tennyson's recent murder, we must consider the new facts in the case.'

It was just after toothbrushes. We were sitting in the airing cupboard, and I was taking notes.

'All right,' said Daisy. 'What new facts do we know? Hazel, write down the list as I say it.

'*One*: Miss Tennyson was murdered in her boarding house, with a large dose of Veronal. So the killer must be someone she knows, and who knows she takes Veronal to help her sleep. Miss Lappet fits that perfectly. On the face of it, The One is less likely, because as a man he wouldn't be allowed past Miss Tennyson's boarding-house matron, but it's possible he sent Miss Hopkins to do it for him. King Henry told me that Miss Griffin keeps medical records for all the masters and mistresses in her office, so any one of our three suspects could have crept in and read Miss Tennyson's.'

So far, this all seemed perfectly right to me.

'*Two*: Miss Tennyson must have been murdered by her accomplice because she was going to tell the police about the crime. Do all three have a motive to work with Miss Tennyson? Miss Lappet is an easy yes. She could have combined forces with Miss Tennyson to knock out their main rival for the Deputy post. Then she'd be doubly eager to get rid of Miss Tennyson afterwards. Miss Hopkins and The One – well, you said it, Hazel. They would have known perfectly well that the Hop would have been sacked as soon as Miss Griffin heard – and Mr Reid too, for being the one who's marrying her – so they might have killed Miss Bell together to stop the news of their engagement getting out, and then roped in Miss Tennyson as a scapegoat.'

I nodded. 'And, you know,' I said, 'even though you were wrong about Miss Tennyson killing Miss Bell on her own, I think you were right about how the murder happened.' If Daisy could admit that I had been right about some things, it only seemed fair that I do the same to her. 'So that means we know how the murderer – or murderers – did it, and when they did it. We only have to work out who it was.'

Daisy beamed. 'Absolutely correct!' she cried. 'Let the police do their worst! We have the most wonderful head start. Tomorrow, we follow our suspects until we learn the truth. And I absolutely promise not to jump to any conclusions unless you agree with me.'

On that note, the meeting was adjourned.

We had narrowed our list down to three suspects, and this time we knew we had to be careful. If we had not caught the real murderer by the end of the week, I decided, then we were no sort of detectives at all.

PART EIGHT

THE DETECTIVE SOCIETY SOLVES THE CASE

1

The next day, Tuesday, the police really *did* arrive. We walked down to school in a biting wind which left my face bright red and raw and turned the end of Daisy's nose a delicate pink. Lavinia, in a cruel mood, tripped Beanie up and spilled her book bag open, and we had to sprint about catching bits of flying paper while Beanie wailed and Kitty comforted her and passing shrimps giggled.

We were brought up short by the sight of a policeman standing in front of Old Wing Entrance. He was in uniform, with a blue buttoned-up jacket and tall blue hat, and as we crept past on our way inside he seemed impossibly severe and awful. The guilt of what I knew we had done to Miss Tennyson went sizzling through me. For a moment *I* felt like the murderer.

We saw another policeman on the way to Prayers. He was much younger than the tall one at Old Wing

Entrance, and he had a thin neck and spots all across his narrow cheeks.

'*Dreamy*,' whispered Kitty.

'You're desperate,' Lavinia told her scornfully.

'Quiet, girls,' said Miss Lappet, on her way past. I flinched when I saw her. She looked worse than ever – red-nosed and with two cardigan buttons gaping open. She squinted at us all and said unsteadily, 'Top buttons done up, if you please.'

As she staggered away, I breathed a little easier. I was still terrified that the murderer might secretly be waiting for the right moment to catch us and add us to their list of victims.

Prayers was very odd. Miss Griffin seemed determined to carry on as though nothing had happened, even though there were now two empty seats where Miss Bell and Miss Tennyson ought to have been. Everyone kept turning round and craning their necks to look at the gaps, and Miss Griffin gave all the turners and craners paralysing stares whenever she caught their eye.

Miss Griffin did mention the police, though. It would have been difficult not to. 'I would like you girls to extend them every courtesy,' she told us sternly, 'while they carry out their investigations, which I'm sure we all hope will be completed as quickly as possible. The sooner this regrettable business is cleared up, the better. And now, the day's notices . . .'

I saw Daisy looking at the spotty policeman thought-fully as we passed him again on the way to Maths. She had her planning expression on, and I suspected that I was about to be asked to do something illegal.

Sure enough, while Miss Parker was writing out sums for us on the blackboard, and looking furious and stiff-haired as she did it, I was slipped a note which read:

At bunbreak go straight for the spotty policeman. I'll do the talking – D.

This sounded suspiciously like there would be no time to collect our biscuits. I did not much like that. Tuesdays are Peek Frean bourbon creams, my favourite. They are even better than gingernuts.

Sure enough, as soon as the bunbreak bell went, Daisy seized my hand and rushed me out of Science, down the stairs and into Library corridor. The spotty policeman was standing next to the mistresses' common-room door, watching the opposite wall with a slightly cross-eyed stare. I looked at him again, and was still unable to understand what Kitty saw in him.

Daisy, however, seemed absolutely charmed. She tugged at her plait until it came loose over her shoulders, dropped her book bag on my feet and then rushed up to the policeman with a very Kitty-like squeal of glee.

'*Oh!*' she exclaimed. 'I've always wanted to meet a policeman!'

Before the spotty policeman had time to realize what was happening to him, she had pounced on his arm and was clinging to it, gazing up at him raptly. He started and a look of panic spread over his spotty face.

'Good morning, Miss,' he said awkwardly. 'What can I do for you?'

Daisy widened her blue eyes at him. 'I think policemen are fascinating,' she said breathlessly. 'All that work you do – it's simply marvellous. Are you a *detective*?'

The spotty policeman coughed. A blotchy flush spread all the way up his thin neck to the tips of his ears.

'Yes, Miss, I am,' he said, and then blushed even more.

'Oh!' gasped Daisy. 'It must be the most wonderful thing in the world. You must be awfully clever.'

'Oh no,' said the policeman. 'Oh no, no, no, not me.'

'Oh, but you are! It's all round the school that you were the one who first realized that this might not be a suicide.'

The policeman's skinny chest puffed out. 'Is it?' he asked squeakily. 'Well, I suppose – see – yes, all right. At first we thought it was just your average – bottle of Veronal by the bed, scrap of writing on her blotter that read "I am so sorry to do this to you". But I noticed something interesting. She was lying so nice on the bed, nightdress done up perfectly, hair brushed, but then there were scratches on her hands, and a little cut on her lip – as though she'd struggled. It didn't add up, and I said so to the chief. Then we went to interview the lady who runs your Miss Tennyson's boarding house, and *she* said someone came to visit her on Saturday, the night she died. A woman.'

My heart jumped. Had it been Miss Lappet or Miss Hopkins?

'Oh!' squealed Daisy, on cue. 'How frightfully exciting!'

The policeman beamed at her. 'Of course,' he said, 'you mustn't tell anyone what I've just told you. It's strictly confidential.'

'Oh yes,' said Daisy. 'Strictly. But – strictly confidential, again – what did she look like, this woman?'

She asked it a little too quickly, and it suddenly sounded strange. I winced inwardly. Daisy tried to cover her mistake by adding, in her silliest voice, 'I mean, was she all *murderous*?'

But even with her charm on, she had gone too far. The policeman blinked and flushed, and then seemed to come out of the spell Daisy had put him under.

'H-here!' he said, stammering. 'What d'you want to know that for? You're going to go round telling all your friends, aren't you?'

'No!'

'You'd better not! This is very privileged information. Oh, I oughtn't to have told you so much about it. Promise me you won't tell anyone else I did? The chief'll have me up for it.'

'Oh, of *course* I won't,' said Daisy, being as reassuring as possible. 'Don't be so silly! I think you're terribly lucky, being in the middle of it like that! Do you know—'

But at that moment a man came out of the mistresses' common room and saw Daisy speaking to the spotty policeman. This man had a long nose, black eyes and thick dark hair slicked back from his forehead. He looked extremely official. In fact, I realized, this must be the police chief the spotty policeman had mentioned.

'Rogers!' the chief said sharply, his face crumpling up in annoyance. 'Don't talk to the young ladies.' He gave Daisy a very nasty glare, and she stared back at him, unmoved.

'Goodbye, Mr Detective,' she said to Rogers, looking up at him through her eyelashes. With one more withering glare at the police chief, she said, 'Come on, Hazel, we must be going now,' and stalked away down Library corridor.

2

Daisy plunged along so fast that I could not keep up with her. I was still puffing along Library corridor when she reached the end and flicked round the corner into New Wing. There was a shriek, a *thump*, then a chorus of horrified gasps, and I heard Daisy's voice, high with panic, crying, 'Oh, I'm so terribly sorry . . . Oh, Miss Griffin – oh, oh, here, let me—'

I dashed round the corner and came face to face with a catastrophe. The corridor was absolutely littered with things – papers and exercise books, hairpins and bull's eyes and pencils – all clattering and rolling about. Daisy, in her haste, had careened straight into the neat and tidy form of Miss Griffin. I gaped in horror.

Daisy was on her knees, frantically scooping things up again. Miss Griffin's carefully set hair was disarranged and her expression was horrible to see. Everyone began to gather round, but Miss Griffin rapped out, 'Move along, girls,' and they all fled in terror.

I got down next to Daisy. She was sliding about over the tiles, picking up papers and stammering, 'Miss Griffin, I am so terribly sorry, please believe me,' but Miss Griffin did not look as though she believed anything much.

I picked up a letter, bending its corner, and Miss Griffin snapped, 'Don't touch that, Wong. Oh, out of the way, both of you, so you don't cause any more damage.' I could tell she was terribly angry. I had never heard her snarl at a girl like that before.

Daisy, trembling, presented Miss Griffin with the pile of papers she had already collected and we both shuffled backwards to begin scooping up the things from Daisy's bag. Miss Griffin, meanwhile, knelt down in her impeccable tweed skirt and gathered up papers as though she was one of Deepdean's maids. It made me burn with shame. I felt as if we had both let the school down terribly. Daisy kept stammering out how sorry she was, but Miss Griffin was in no mood to listen.

'Wells, *enough*. This does not become you at all. Deepdean girls should accept the blame for their mistakes with the same grace and quiet dignity that they show in the rest of their lives. I do not expect to see my girls tearing about the school like barbarians. Quite frankly, I am disappointed in you. You may go.'

'Yes, Miss Griffin,' said Daisy weakly, and she curt-seyed, though slightly lopsidedly, because she had the contents of her book bag loose in her arms. Then we both scuttled away, feeling like the smallest of small shrimps.

'I thought I was for it,' Daisy whispered to me once we were far enough down the corridor. 'Oh Lord, though, look at the time. We shall be fearfully late for Art.'

We looked round once more, to make sure that Miss Griffin was not watching us (she wasn't – she had just bent down to pick up something else), and then we ran for it.

I always enjoy Art. This is less to do with the Art itself, and more to do with the fact that to The One, Hong Kong is part of a magical, made-up place called The Orient; because I am from there, he thinks I must be a natural artist. He seems to imagine that everyone in Hong Kong lies about on bright purple divans, in rooms papered with that Chinese print you can get in Woolworth's, with peacocks wandering about at our feet. Of course this is not true, and I am not a natural artist at all, but The One hasn't noticed. So I copy Chinese dragons out of books I find in the library, and The One is delighted.

That day I was busily colouring in one of my dragons when I noticed that Daisy had stopped work and was scrabbling about in her book bag with an awful expression on her face.

'Is something wrong?' I whispered.

In answer, Daisy took her bag and tipped the whole thing up over her desk. Pencils, rubbers and bits of string rained down, and Daisy began to hunt through them, picking each thing up and then tossing it aside again a moment later.

'Hazel,' she said, still hunting away frantically, 'Hazel, *I can't find the earring.*'

I went cold. 'Are you sure?'

'Of course I'm sure,' Daisy hissed, gesturing at the contents of her bag. There certainly was no gold earring to be seen.

My last look back at Miss Griffin played like a film-reel in my head. She had been bending down over something small lying on the tiles, looking at it intently. I glanced at Daisy, and saw that she was having exactly the same thought as me.

'What shall we do?' she gasped. 'Miss Griffin will put it straight into Davey Jones.' *Davey Jones* is our name for Miss Griffin's box of confiscated items. It sits in her office and we call it that because you know that once something's gone in there you'll never see it again. 'We'll never get it back. How will we confront our suspects if we don't have the earring? Oh, Hazel, our beautiful case. It's ruined!'

'Well,' I said, surprising myself by what came out of my mouth next, 'if we need it, we'll just have to get it back. We'll go to Miss Griffin's office at lunch and you can tell her that it's a present for your mother, or something. It's worth a try, anyway. After all, Miss Griffin likes you.'

'She did until I ran into her half an hour ago,' said Daisy. 'But still, it's an excellent idea, Hazel! Whatever has got into you?'

'I want to solve the case,' I said. 'I want the person who killed Miss Bell and Miss Tennyson punished. You said yourself how important it was.'

Daisy raised her eyebrows. 'Yes, but – Hazel Wong, encouraging *me* to tell a lie! I never thought I'd see the day. You're right, though. We need that earring, and we're going to get it back!'

3

Daisy and I made for Miss Griffin's office, on the top floor of New Wing, at the end of lunch. We should not really have been in New Wing out of lesson time, of course, but things were still so mixed up after Miss Tennyson's death that no one had time to notice us running by except the dark-haired chief of police, who gave us a *look* as we passed him on our way up the stairs by the founder's portrait. I hoped we were looking innocent.

The door to Miss Griffin's office was closed. Daisy and I grimaced at each other encouragingly and then Daisy knocked on the door. My heart was hammering as we waited to hear Miss Griffin's voice, but the person who answered our knock was not Miss Griffin at all. It was Miss Lappet.

'Come in!' she called, and there was a hurried clinking noise. Daisy and I looked at each other in a panic. Neither of us had expected this. Asking Miss Griffin for the earring was terrifying enough, but asking one of our three remaining suspects for the evidence that might prove that she had done it – that was more frightening altogether.

'Come in!' Miss Lappet called again, and this time her voice was tinged with annoyance.

'We'll just have to bluff it!' Daisy whispered to me. 'This could be a way to finally eliminate her!'

Or prove that she did the murders, I thought. I was about to tell Daisy not to go in, but she was already pushing open the door.

Daisy is a marvellous actress, and at that moment I was glad. My heart was drumming painfully in my chest, and my knees were wobbling, but Daisy behaved as though nothing was wrong at all. 'Oh! Miss Lappet!' she said, as though it was a jolly surprise. 'Good afternoon!'

'Good afternoon, Daisy, Hazel,' said Miss Lappet. She was at the desk where Miss Bell used to work, next to Miss Griffin's big green leather one, and she was squinting at us. Her grey hair was fluffy, her glasses were askew and there was a stain on her enormous blouse front. She looked a harmless fright. But appearances, I had learned, could be deceptive. I made sure to stop a safe distance away from her, halfway across Miss Griffin's green and blue patterned carpet, and let Daisy speak.

'Miss Lappet,' she said, 'this is a terribly awful thing

to ask of you. I really ought to wait until Miss Griffin comes back – it's a rather difficult request—'

That got to Miss Lappet, of course.

'As you can see, today I am acting as Miss Griffin's secretary while she deals with the police. Anything you can say to Miss Griffin, you can say to me, dear,' she said.

'Oh!' Daisy said, 'In that case . . . I'm sure Miss Griffin told you that I bumped into her this morning. I feel like such an imbecile, I shall *never* forgive myself for it, but – well, I dropped something when I crashed into her. It was something I oughtn't to have had, but Mummy's birthday is next week. I know it was terribly wrong of me to have her present down at school, and as soon as I found it was missing I realized that the only thing to do was come to Miss Griffin and simply beg her to let me have it back.'

'How sweet,' said Miss Lappet, slurring the W slightly. 'What was it, exactly?'

I braced myself, feeling as though I was about to be tackled by a very large Big Girl wielding a hockey stick.

'Well, I bought Mummy a pair of gold earrings, but when I looked in Art I could only find one of them still in their box. It's two long teardrops, one above the other.'

I waited for Miss Lappet to jump up from her seat and shout, or faint, or hurl Miss Griffin's paperweight at us. Instead, she merely looked confused. 'But, Daisy dear, what an odd coincidence. How strange. Are you sure? Miss Griffin has just found her own earring that has been missing all week – a gold one just like that. She showed it to me a minute ago, and here it is still in her desk.'

And she took something out of one of the desk's many drawers and held it out for us to see. There on her palm sat the earring that we had found in the tunnel, its two gold tears shining. 'You see, this is Miss Griffin's, dear,' Miss Lappet told Daisy. 'Are you sure the earring you lost was like this one?'

Daisy blinked. Then she said, very quickly, 'Oh no, you're right. How annoying! I'm terribly sorry to have bothered you. Come along, Hazel, we ought to be going. I'm sure Miss Lappet is very busy. Come *along*, Hazel.'

She had to drag me out of the room. I couldn't take my eyes off the gold earring in Miss Lappet's hand. *It couldn't be*, I thought, *It couldn't be!* But it was. There the earring sat, looking ordinary as anything, except that what it meant was something utterly terrible.

Miss Lappet was not the murderer.

Neither were Miss Hopkins or The One.

It was *Miss Griffin*.

4

Miss Griffin had done it. Why hadn't we thought of her as a suspect?

Daisy had me by the wrist. She was dragging me along somewhere, and I let her. I didn't much care about anything except what was going on in my head.

Miss Griffin had done it. Of course, as soon as we knew that Miss Lappet's supposed alibi was useless, we should have realized that Miss Griffin's had vanished as well – but we had never even considered her. I thought again about that conversation Daisy had overheard between Miss Griffin and Miss Tennyson. Why hadn't we realized how sinister Miss Griffin's request had been?

There I was, minding my own business in an opportune listening place in Library corridor, Daisy had told me, *and Miss Griffin came up to Miss Tennyson. 'Miss Tennyson,' she said, 'I need to talk to you. You haven't quite finished helping me with that little project of ours. You were so late* to my office on Monday evening that we barely got a thing done.'

'Yes, but I made up for it on Tuesday and Wednesday,' Miss Tennyson had said nervously.

'Ah, but not quite,' replied Miss Griffin. 'There's still just a bit of work that needs to be finished.'

Honestly, Hazel, Miss Tennyson went as white as a sheet. She was shaking. 'Can we perhaps schedule another session?' asked Miss Griffin. 'There's just a little more work I'd like you to do – perhaps this evening?'

If it had been any other mistress, we might have been more suspicious. But somehow Miss Griffin had always seemed so remote from the other masters and mistresses, so above everything that went on at Deepdean. And Miss Lappet, Miss Hopkins and The One had all been such good suspects – so had Miss Tennyson and Miss Parker, to start with. They'd all had motives for killing Miss Bell, while Miss Griffin didn't appear to have any motive at all.

But Miss Griffin *had* done it. *Why?*

I felt Daisy shaking my arm.

'Hazel,' she said. 'You're talking to yourself.'

I blinked, and found that somehow we had ended up in Old Wing cloakroom. The bell for the end of lunch break was ringing.

'Come on,' said Daisy. 'Hide.'

She dragged me into one of the very far corners,

which was full of the coats that girls from years ago lost and never bothered to find again. They smelled slightly rotten, and their grey fabric had gone a bit green with age.

I squeezed myself in next to Daisy. We sat there in the dimness, trying not to breathe in the old coat smell too much. Then Daisy reached out her hand and took hold of mine. I could feel it shaking.

'I never guessed it would be Miss Griffin,' she said quietly. 'I didn't want to tell you, but I was nearly sure that it was Miss Hopkins and The One. It was all beginning to fit – motive, means, even the earring. But – oh, Miss Griffin!'

I nodded, making the coats in front of my face sway. 'She doesn't seem real, does she?' I asked.

'She isn't human,' said Daisy. 'She's a Headmistress through and through. I thought so, anyway. Well! Now we know how the murderer got Miss Tennyson to help – Miss Griffin must have offered the Deputy job in exchange for her services. And that conversation I overheard on Friday makes sense now! Miss Griffin was reminding Miss Tennyson that they were in it together; she must have been asking her to help search the school again that evening, for the lost earring! The torch we saw when we were creeping about on Friday night – well, I suppose that must have been *them*, hunting. Heavens.

'I wonder why she did it, though? What on earth

would be worth murdering two people for, if you are already the Headmistress of Deepdean? Miss Tennyson had to be bumped off because she was on the verge of telling the police, but why ever kill Miss Bell in the first place?'

'She must have had a reason,' I said, although my mind was as blank as Daisy's. Miss Griffin seemed to have everything, to want for nothing. She ruled Deepdean, had all the other mistresses running after her, was perfectly well-off, and even quite good looking, for an old person. 'I don't know what, though,' I admitted.

'Let's be logical about this,' said Daisy, squeezing my hand. Hers was beginning to feel more steady, although mine was still trembling. 'We know she did it. Just as you said, we know when and how. Now all we need is to know why. Why do people kill other people?'

'Money,' I said promptly. Daisy has drummed these reasons into me enough times for me to know them by heart. 'Power. Love. Fear. Revenge. But Miss Griffin had more money and power than Miss Bell anyway, so it can't have been those.'

'Likewise,' said Daisy, 'revenge seems unlikely. Miss Griffin could have simply not given Miss Bell the Deputy job, or fired her, if she wanted revenge for something. So that leaves Love and Fear. Well, what if – Hazel, tell me if this doesn't make sense – what if Miss Bell was blackmailing Miss Griffin? Asking for money – or, no, the Deputy job – in exchange for keeping quiet about something? That would explain why Miss Griffin couldn't simply fire Miss Bell.'

'But Miss Griffin seems so perfect!' I objected. 'What could she be blackmailed about?'

'Well, I don't know,' said Daisy, 'but if she's killed two people over it, it must be rather awful. What do you think, though? Am I right?'

Even then, in the middle of everything else going on in my head, I had time to be amazed. Daisy Wells, asking me what I thought about her detective work!

'It does make sense,' I said. 'If anything does.'

'Pity we can't just ask Miss Bell about it, isn't it?' asked Daisy with a little chuckle. 'Excuse me, but *why* were you murdered?'

'Perhaps she left a note,' I said.

Daisy chuckled again. Then she squeezed my fingers so hard that I yelped.

'Hazel,' she said, 'that isn't actually a stupid thing to say *at all*. As all my books point out, blackmailers do generally keep copies of incriminating documents in a safe place for insurance. What if Miss Bell did something like that?'

'If she did,' I said, squeezing back in excitement, 'they might be down at school.'

'*Yes!*' said Daisy. 'I bet Miss Griffin and Miss Tennyson were looking for them *as well* as the earring last week!'

Then we both remembered that Deepdean was rather a large place. We sank back into the coats, sighing.

'No, wait,' said Daisy, sitting upright again. 'Let's deduce. Miss Bell and Miss Griffin must have prearranged their meeting in the Gym – they wouldn't have met there by chance on a Monday evening. So Miss Bell would have had time to prepare for it – and hide any evidence she was using to blackmail Miss Griffin. She would have put it somewhere safe, somewhere Miss Griffin wouldn't have thought of when she was looking for it.'

'So not the mistresses' common room,' I said. 'And not the science labs, either.'

'Too obvious,' Daisy agreed. 'Well, where do we know Miss Bell went on Monday night?'

'The Gym,' I said. 'But there's nowhere to hide something in the Gym. Jones would find it if it was in the Cupboard, and besides, it's too close to the meeting place.'

Then, in a flash of something that Daisy would have called Sherlocky brilliance if it had happened to her, I saw the answer. 'Daisy,' I breathed. '*The cloakroom.* Right here! Remember the first former who found Miss Bell digging about behind the coats in here? We only used what she said to establish when Miss Bell left for the Gym, but what if Miss Bell was here to hide her evidence?'

Daisy said something extremely unladylike. Then she hugged me. I glowed.

'Coat pockets!' she cried. 'Nobody ever uses these ratty old ones, they stay here until they rot away! It's the perfect hiding place! Quick, Hazel, dig!'

And she began pawing through the pile of old coats that surrounded us.

Shivering with excitement, I hunted with her. We were on the trail again, I thought, as I shoved my hand into ripped and dirty pockets, pulling out snapped pencils and coat-furry sweets. Then my fingertips bumped against something large and cardboard-stiff that crackled when I squeezed it.

Holding my breath, I pulled it out and parted the coats in front of me to see that I was clutching a red notebook that said, in small precise letters on its cover,

VERITY'S DIARY.

'Daisy,' I said quietly. 'I've got it.'

5

Daisy gave a whoop of triumph – but I couldn't get past those two carefully inked words.

I got a chill all the way down my spine. *Verity Abraham.* She seemed to be everywhere. I know it sounds stupid, but at that moment I really *did* wonder if she was haunting me. I imagined her with her hanging-down hair and her bloodstained clothes and a hot-and-cold shiver ran through me.

Daisy didn't see it that way at all. 'Goodness,' she said, peering at the book. 'Verity. I say, that's Verity Abraham!'

'I know,' I said shakily. It was funny to think that before Verity became my ghost girl she had been a real, ordinary schoolgirl at Deepdean, who ate biscuits and kept a diary. I took a deep breath, bent the spine open, and began to read.

25th September 1933

The beginning of another year! And such
an important year too. Daddy keeps on
reminding me that this is the year I begin to
prepare for my university entrance exam.
It is terribly important, I know, and I am
lucky enough to be coached by Miss Griffin
herself! I am amazed to have been chosen
by her. I always thought — well, I'm ashamed
to say it now, but I always assumed that
she did not like me very much. She always
seemed to avoid me in the corridors. So
I was simply amazed to be told that she
had requested me specially! I have made a
resolution to buck up and work as hard as I
possibly can, so as to be worthy of her.

'Boring,' said Daisy. 'Skim to the racy bit. What?
There must *be* one!'

18th October 1933

The exam prep is going – I wish I could say well. I hope it is. I am certainly doing my best, though I fear I am a little slow at times. But I am becoming more and more puzzled by Miss Griffin. She is behaving so *oddly*. She always seems to be on the verge of saying – *something* – and when she is coaching me, certain things make her peculiarly twitchy. We were discussing Jocasta, that mad lady who abandoned her son, Oedipus, and Miss Griffin kept on trying to justify what she did! I did not quite like to disagree with her, since she is the Headmistress, but really! I wonder if she is quite all right.

24th October 1933

I am beginning to suspect that Miss Griffin has some sort of secret! In fact, I think she has a dark secret in her past. I told Henry the other day, and she thinks it's tosh, but I believe I am right. I wonder what it can be?

16th November 1933

I simply can't be mistaken any more. Miss Griffin has a secret — and I believe she is on the verge of revealing it to me! I feel quite honoured, although I do hope it isn't something horrible. Anyway, she keeps giving me the oddest looks, and half saying things . . . I said all this to Henry, and she said I was batty, that everyone knows mistresses don't have secrets, or at least not important ones. Henry is so *boring* sometimes.

20th November 1933

I was right. But, oh Lord — what shall I do? It simply can't be. But it is. She showed me all the documents . . . she had them all laid out — she seemed to be hoping— Wait, I am not being methodical about this account. Let me begin again.

Tonight, during our tutoring session, Miss Griffin finally told me her secret. Seventeen years ago, before she came to Deepdean,

when she was a mistress at another school – she had a baby. She was not married, and so of course it was hushed up. The baby was given away to a very nice family.
That baby was me.

I stopped reading with a gasp, and Daisy gave an undignified squeal. 'Really!' she cried. 'Really! Oh, Hazel, *excitement*!'

I couldn't believe it, but then she showed me all the certificates, with my parents' signatures and her own. It really is true. Oh Lord, what shall I do? Mummy is not my mummy any more, and Daddy is no relation to me either – instead, I'm the daughter of a schoolmistress. A schoolmistress! A nobody, and not even married!

What shall I do? I think she wanted me to leap into her arms and call her *Mother*. Of course, I couldn't. I ran out of her office – I don't ever want to go back.

21st November 1933

I told Henry what had happened. She couldn't believe it either. She says I should wait before I tell anyone else, but I don't see why. How could Miss Griffin do this to me? I want to talk to Mummy and Daddy, and make them say that it is all a lie.

22nd November 1933

Miss Griffin wants me to stay quiet too. I think she's alarmed by my reaction. I don't see why she should have expected anything different. She says I have to consider her position, that it should be our secret. But what about *my* position? This is not fair of her!

23rd November 1933

Note from Miss Griffin today, asking me to come and see her on the Gym balcony after the end of school, to 'discuss the situation'. I have stuck it in this book, just in case of — oh, I don't know what. I will go, but it shan't change my mind. I *will* talk to Mummy and Daddy about it when I go home for the hols. She can't stop me. She can't tell me what to do.

And that was the last thing Verity wrote in her diary.

But it wasn't the last thing in the diary itself. When Daisy shook it, two pieces of paper fell out.

The first was a short note, in Miss Griffin's beautiful copperplate.

Miss Abraham.

I request your company on the Gym balcony at 5.30 this evening. the 23rd November. to discuss the situation between us. Please do not be late.

Rosemary Griffin

The second was in Miss Bell's angular handwriting.

To whom it may concern.

I have evidence to prove that the Headmistress of Deepdean School for Girls, Rosemary Griffin, caused the death of her pupil Verity Abraham in November of 1933. Whether Miss Griffin attacked Verity with the intention of ending her life, or whether it was a tragic accident, I do not know, but the enclosed diary and note together prove that she was present at the moment of Verity's death, and that she caused the incident by revealing to Verity that she was her natural mother. Rosemary Griffin is not fit to hold the post of Headmistress any longer. She should be immediately removed from her position at Deepdean, and I submit myself for consideration as her replacement.

Joan Bell, Monday 29th October 1934

'Fancy!' said Daisy gleefully. 'I'd say that was a motive for murder, all right. It looks like Miss Bell got greedy and wanted to force Miss Griffin out of Deepdean alto-gether. She'd have lost everything! Oh, if the school only knew!'

I was glowing pink with shock. I could barely take it in. Miss Griffin, the great Miss Griffin, had been involved in a shameful affair, and, as a result of this, had a *baby*. It was not the sort of thing that respectable school-mistresses did! And Verity had been her daughter! *Had* Miss Griffin killed Verity on purpose, so that she would not talk? Or had it just been an accident? Whatever the truth was, Verity had not committed suicide at all. The person who had written that diary would never have killed herself. So it must have been Miss Griffin's fault. The thought made my skin crawl with horror.

Something occurred to me then. 'The Henry that Verity mentioned – that's King Henry, isn't it? So she's known all the time! That must be why she's been looking so odd, and why she was coming to speak to Miss Tennyson at the Willow. I knew she had something to do with this!'

Daisy nodded. 'She can't have known exactly what was going on, but I bet she suspected. Perhaps she real-ized that Miss Tennyson had something to do with it, and that's why she was going to meet her on Saturday. But the important thing is that we've got all the evidence we need to accuse Miss Griffin. Whatever she says now, we've got her. Hazel, we've solved the case.'

'Miss Bell solved the case,' I said.

'Don't be an idiot, Hazel,' said Daisy. 'She's dead. She didn't solve anything.'

I was just opening my mouth to argue – or perhaps to say something else about the extraordinary things we had discovered – when the cloakroom door creaked open.

6

Daisy and I both froze. You see, that was all wrong. It was the middle of a lesson (one which Daisy and I were missing), and so no one should have been wandering around school grounds so quietly.

Luckily we were still hidden behind our rack of discarded coats, at the very back of the room. No one looking in could see us – and that was what saved us.

The door opened all the way, there was a moment of utter silence, and then Miss Griffin said, 'Daisy? Hazel? Where are you, girls?'

I could feel Daisy's hand gripping mine, and hear our breathing and our hearts. They sounded as loud as shouting, and I was shaking so hard that I imagined Miss Griffin seeing clouds of dust flying up off the coats around us.

She had come to find us. She knew! Miss Lappet must have told her we had been looking for the earring. She was going to kill us, I thought frantically, and then bury us next to Miss Bell out in the woods and tell our parents that we had run away!

I thought I had been afraid of the murderer before, during our investigation, but I never knew until that moment how much I did not want to be dead.

'Girls?' called Miss Griffin again. 'Girls, are you in there? Come on out, I've got a lovely surprise for you!'

I could not have felt more terrified if she had said, *Come out so I can murder you*!

'Miss Lappet told me that there'd been a misunderstanding. She gave you a wrong impression earlier. Come out, girls, and I can explain.'

It felt so strange to disobey a mistress. But we did not come out.

At last, Miss Griffin sighed. She pulled the door to, and the room was quiet again.

I was about to jump out of our hiding place, but Daisy hissed, 'Wait!'

We waited, and waited, and *then* we heard Miss Griffin's footsteps moving away.

Daisy collapsed against me, shaking. 'Quick!' she cried. 'We have to get to lessons before she comes back!'

'Really?' I asked doubtfully. My knees were like wet jelly. I wasn't sure I wanted to move at all.

'Do you want to wait for her here?' asked Daisy.

I shook my head.

Once we'd left the cloakroom I felt as though I had a spotlight trained on my head. I expected Miss Griffin to pounce on us at any second. I was clutching Verity's diary to my chest like a shield, and when we turned a corner and almost walked into the dark-haired police chief coming the other way, I jumped so hard my teeth chattered.

Daisy shied away from him, and I realized with horror that, despite what had happened, she still wanted to finish the case without help from the police – even though Miss Griffin might be just round the next corner, waiting to catch us. It only took me a moment to decide that it was time for me to stop behaving like a secretary, or even a second in command. It was up to me to save us.

The policeman was already turning away.

'Excuse me,' I said. 'Wait! We need your help.'

The policeman turned to face me. 'Yes?' he asked politely.

'Hazel!' cried Daisy. 'What are you *doing*?'

I ought to have felt guilty. But once again, I did not feel guilty at all.

'Please help us,' I said in a rush. 'We know who killed Miss Tennyson. It was Miss Griffin, and she's killed our Science mistress Miss Bell as well, and now she's coming after us! *Please!*'

I could tell that he did not believe me. He frowned, and his face crinkled up with it. 'I'm terribly sorry,' he said, 'but what are you talking about?'

'Miss Griffin is the murderer,' I said. 'It's true! *Look!* We've got evidence!'

And I thrust Verity's diary at his chest.

'Hazel!' Daisy shouted again. '*Don't!*'

But the policeman was already flicking through it. At first he was only doing it to be polite – but then his eyebrows shot up, and his forehead wrinkled, and he began to turn over the pages more quickly.

'Where did you get this?' he asked.

'Oh, never mind that!' I said. 'You have to help us! Miss Griffin is after us! She wants to kill us!'

For one awful moment I thought that he was going to turn us away. But instead, he took a deep breath, put his big hands on our shoulders, steered us towards the door of the nearest form room and pushed us inside.

The policeman had saved us from Miss Griffin. I could have hugged him. Daisy, of course, was less pleased. I didn't even need to look at her to know that she was about to be difficult.

'All right,' said the policeman, turning to us with an extremely serious expression on his face. 'What's all this about?'

Daisy sniffed. 'Hazel's said too much already,' she said, folding her arms and wrinkling her nose up. 'I don't see why I should tell you any more. Who *are* you, anyway? You've been here all day and you haven't even introduced yourself.'

I was horrified in case the policeman sent us back outside, but to my great relief Daisy's speech seemed only to amuse him.

'I am Inspector Priestley,' he told us. 'And you are?'

'*I* am Daisy Wells, daughter of Lord Hastings,' said Daisy, as though she were the Queen, 'and this is my friend Hazel Wong. And this is *our* murder case and we've solved it without you, thank you very much. No matter what Hazel says, we don't need your help.'

The Inspector raised his eyebrows at that, so that his whole forehead wrinkled up again. 'Do you mean to say that you have more than the diary you've shown me?' he asked. 'You can prove what Hazel has just told me about Miss Griffin?'

Daisy squirmed. I could tell that she was having a terrible inner struggle over whether to reveal our cleverness to the Inspector.

But I did not want to face a murderous Miss Griffin on my own. We had solved the case, and now there was nothing more we could do. As much as Daisy hated it, we had to tell the police what we knew.

'Yes!' I said. 'We know that Miss Griffin killed Miss Bell. Miss Bell was blackmailing her over what had happened with Verity Abraham last year, you see. It's all in the diary. Miss Bell must have found it while she was doing Miss Griffin's secretary work earlier this year. So Miss Griffin killed Miss Bell to silence her, and made Miss Tennyson help her dispose of the body. Then she killed Miss Tennyson too, because *she* was planning to go to the police. *And* she tried to kill us just now! I know it sounds mad, but we can prove it. We've got evidence. Show him, Daisy.'

Daisy, after another moment's wriggling, stuck her hand into her bag, pulled out the stained gym slip, the piece of string and the bit of Miss Bell's lab coat, and said, 'Oh, all right! But I hope you'll remember later that *we* found these.'

And then we both explained the whole of our investigation to the policeman. I found that once I had started, I couldn't stop, though Daisy kept on butting in with better explanations. We told him about losing the earring – 'Our most important piece of evidence!' said Daisy furiously – and how tracking it down had led us to Miss Griffin. I could tell that the Inspector was only listening politely at first, but as Daisy and I talked, he took a notebook out of his coat pocket and began to write in it. His face became more and more crumpled, and his eyebrows moved higher and higher up his forehead.

When we had finished he put his pen down, rubbed his hand over his face, and laughed.

'Not bad for your Detective Society's first murder case,' he said.

'You believe us?' said Daisy sharply.

'You present a compelling, if slightly muddled, account of events. It's rather difficult not to believe you. It's a pity you don't have that earring any more, but I'm sure I can close the case without it.'

Daisy made a face at *muddled*, but I was relieved.

'And you'll look for Miss Bell's body?' I asked.

'Yes, I'll send my men out to Oakeshott Woods this afternoon. But until I wrap up the case' – his face became serious again – 'I need to keep you safe from Miss Griffin. I don't like the thought of the two of you roaming about carrying on your Young Miss Marple routine while she's still a free woman.'

'Miss Marple!' hissed Daisy under her breath. 'Holmes and Watson, *if* you please.'

'Is there anywhere you can go for a few hours?' asked Inspector Priestley, pretending he had not heard.

'We could go to Nurse Minn in San,' I offered.

The Inspector nodded. 'Good. You can stay there until Miss Griffin's been arrested. I'll keep one of my men guarding you and put another on her tail. Remember – no heroics! You've already done quite enough.'

'Well, we *did* solve your case for you,' said Daisy.

The Inspector got up from his chair and smoothed down his dark hair. 'Indeed you did, Madam Super,' he said – which I think must have been a joke at Daisy's expense, only she was too pleased to notice it.

'Thank you,' she said, and she put out her hand for the Inspector to take. He shook it very solemnly (I was now more certain than ever that he was not being entirely serious), and then turned and held out his hand to me. I shook it, feeling suddenly rather shy. I looked up at him out of the corner of my eye and had a shock when I caught him winking at me. I dropped his hand, horribly embarrassed, but when I looked at him again his expression was as polite as ever.

7

When we were safely in San (Nurse Minn took one fluttery look at the Inspector and made no objections at all to us becoming patients), tucked into two cool white beds next to each other, I suddenly felt very much like crying. I stared up at the ceiling and gulped as quietly as I could into my handkerchief while I shivered all over, as though I really was ill.

Beside me Daisy was gabbling away, of course.

'Do you think we'll get a bravery medal from the police? We *were* brave, weren't we?'

'Very,' I said, my teeth chattering. Water kept leaking out of the sides of my eyes in the most shameful manner.

'I say!' said Daisy, noticing me. 'Are you all right, Watson?'

'Yes!' I said, my teeth chattering all the more. 'I'm quite all right. Only – I can't stop—'

And I burst into tears.

'Hazel!' cried Daisy, and quick as a flash she leaped out of her bed and hurled herself onto mine. 'Oh, poor Hazel!'

'I'm sorry!' I stuttered. 'I'm not – behaving – very much like a detective.'

'Hazel,' said Daisy, putting her arms round my shoulders and leaning her forehead against mine, 'don't talk nonsense. Throughout this case, you have behaved like the most splendid detective in the world. In fact, because of your heroic and intelligent actions in The Case of the Murder of Miss Bell I am going to promote you. From this moment on you are the Vice-President of the Detective Society.'

I gulped. 'Really?' I asked.

'*Really*,' said Daisy. 'Now for heaven's sake, stop crying and start thinking about how to get past our police guard.'

That made me stop crying at once.

'What?' I asked. 'But we're safe here!'

'Who wants to be *safe*?' asked Daisy scornfully. 'I want to see the Inspector arrest Miss Griffin.'

I was not sure I did. I felt cushioned by the lovely soft quiet of San, and terrified at the very thought of going back out into a school where Miss Griffin was still on the lookout for us.

But Daisy, for all her changes in the past few weeks,

was still Daisy, and her mad plans were as mad as ever.

'Yes, but how?' I asked.

'Wait,' said Daisy. 'I'm thinking of a plan.'

Then, outside the main San door, we heard voices.

'Come on!' hissed Daisy. 'Let's go and see who it is!'

As soon as we went out of our little room onto the small San landing, where Minny's examination room and all the sickrooms open out into, we could hear that it was two policemen. The one guarding San must have been joined by another, and they were talking.

'. . . having a meeting now,' said the first policeman as we crept up to the closed main door to the corridor and pressed our ears against it to listen. 'The chief's idea. Wants to get her to confess.'

'Trust him to go for drama,' said the other. 'Nice touch, though, I admit. Where are they?'

'That music room, down the other end of the school. I'm off there now as reinforcement. You ought to come.'

'Don't I wish I could!' said our policeman. 'But I'm on nanny duty. Little madams can't get hurt – his orders.'

Daisy flushed with annoyance. 'All right,' she said to me. 'An excellent plan has just come into my brain. Wait here.'

She turned and ran into the other San sick room,

and came back a moment later dragging a small shrimp behind her. It was Binny.

'What are you doing here?' I asked.

'Got a bad stomach,' said Binny. Daisy glared at her. 'Not really – I just wanted to get out of Latin.'

'Don't I know it,' said Daisy. 'And if you want me to keep mum for you, there's something I need you to do.'

'What?' asked Binny.

'When I tell you,' said Daisy, 'I want you to *scream.*'

8

The landing outside San had gone quiet. The other policeman must have gone off to the meeting in the music room. 'Ready?' whispered Daisy. We were crouching just behind the door. Binny, positioned in the very middle of the San hallway, nodded.

'Three, two, one,' whispered Daisy. 'Scream!'

Binny screamed.

It sounded like an express train howling through a tunnel. There was a yell of shock from the policeman out on the landing, and then he came bursting through the door, leaving it wide open and the landing beyond clear.

With Binny's screams still ringing in our ears, Daisy and I ran for it.

We scurried along the corridor towards Music Wing, but just as we were coming to the end of Library corridor I looked behind us and saw the one sight I was hoping like anything that we would avoid.

Miss Griffin was following us.

Daisy clutched my arm in panic, and I clutched at Daisy – and at that moment Miss Griffin realized that she had been seen. The most awful expression came over her face, a *pounce* like a cat on two mice, and she began to stride purposefully towards us.

'Quick!' hissed Daisy. 'RUN!'

And, ignoring all the rules of Deepdean, we ran like hares down New Wing corridor.

I have never been so terrified in my life. I remember galloping along in a sweating awful panic, hearing our feet on the marble tiles – and behind them, the *click, click, click* of Miss Griffin's shoes as she came after us. My heart was burning and hammering in my chest and my ankle throbbed along with it.

'Girls!' called Miss Griffin after us. 'Come here at once! I want to talk to you! You are missing lessons without permission!'

'Ignore her!' panted Daisy.

I did not need to be told twice.

But then we turned the corner into Music Wing and almost crashed into Inspector Priestley.

He was standing in the hallway, a sheaf of papers in his large hands, and at that moment he seemed like the Angel Gabriel or one of the godlike Inspectors from Daisy's novels, descended to earth to save our souls.

'Help!' gasped Daisy, gesturing behind us. 'Miss Griffin!'

The Inspector acted at once.

'Quick!' he said. 'In there!' And he ushered us – or rather, almost shoved us – through the open door of the small music room, before slamming it shut.

He was only just in time. As we leaned against each other, panting as quietly as we could, I heard the clicking of Miss Griffin's shoes once again. They hurried closer and closer – and then stopped. She must have seen the Inspector, I thought.

'Ah, Miss Griffin,' Inspector Priestley said, as though it was the most natural thing in the world that they should meet there. 'You're just in time for our meeting.'

'What meeting?' asked Miss Griffin, sounding extremely ungracious.

'Didn't my sergeant let you know? I'm terribly sorry. I've asked several of the mistresses to meet me here to discuss some developments in the case. In fact, now that you've arrived, we can begin. They're all waiting for you in the music room.'

'Inspector, I am busy. I am looking for two of my pupils. You didn't see two girls pass by here just now, did you?'

I tensed up.

'Ah yes, I did,' said the Inspector. 'They went out of North Entrance in a terrible hurry, I think you've lost them. At least you still have the meeting to console you.'

There was a pause.

'Oh, very well, then,' said Miss Griffin, with bad grace.

I breathed a very quiet sigh of relief.

There was the sound of a door opening and closing, silence outside in the hallway and voices next door to us.

Now, Daisy and I had been shoved into the small music room. It is separate from the big music room, but the two rooms connect by a door, covered with a heavy velvet curtain on the big music room side. Between the door and the curtain there's a narrow little space – just big enough for two girl detectives to squeeze into.

I do wonder whether the Inspector had planned on us listening in. It may have just been a nice coincidence – he never said anything about it to us afterwards – but all the same, Daisy and I opened the connecting door, and slipped in behind the curtain. So we heard exactly what went on at Inspector Priestley's meeting.

9

Daisy and I positioned ourselves one at each end of the curtain, so that we could peep round it into the room beyond. I squashed my cheek against the shivery-cold stone of the alcove wall and had a splendid view of the music room – with its high, white ceiling, and long, curved picture window that looks out onto the lawns and pond. The tall, severe policeman from Old Entrance was backed up against the far wall, looking official, and several hard classroom chairs had been set out in a semicircle facing the big window. Miss Lappet, Miss Hopkins, The One, Miss Parker and Mamzelle were sitting uncomfortably in these chairs, and standing in front of them just like a master in front of his form, was Inspector Priestley. Miss Griffin was still being ushered into an empty chair by Rogers, the spotty policeman. She looked put out, and he looked frankly terrified of her. I didn't blame him.

'Is all this strictly necessary?' snapped Miss Griffin. 'I do have a school to run, you know.'

'I am quite aware of that,' said the Inspector. 'However, it could not be avoided. I do promise that I'll try to take up as little of your time as I can.

'Now, I have called this meeting because of certain developments in my investigation of the death of Miss Tennyson. But I have been made aware that this is not the only unfortunate event Deepdean has suffered recently. You are currently missing your Science mistress, are you not?'

I saw Miss Parker's shoulders shake. I felt a surge of pity for her – she must have been nearly frantic with worry about Miss Bell.

'I am not sure *missing* is the correct word,' said Miss Griffin acidly. 'I received Miss Bell's resignation on my desk last Tuesday morning in the proper manner. She has left the school, and I wish her good luck. Surely that has no bearing on Miss Tennyson's unfortunate suicide?'

The Inspector sighed. 'I am afraid,' he said, 'that the whereabouts of Miss Bell have a great deal to do with this investigation. I am also afraid that those whereabouts are no longer in any doubt. Miss Bell did not resign last Monday at all. Nor did she leave school grounds of her own volition.'

'What do you mean?' cried Miss Parker.

'I mean,' said the Inspector, 'that this afternoon my men discovered a body in Oakeshott Woods; a body that exactly matches the description I have of Miss Bell.'

Miss Parker made a noise that sounded like all the air rushing out of a balloon. Her face had gone red and her mouth was open and gaping fishily, and she clutched at the sides of her chair until her knuckles went red and white in strips.

'The discovery means that this is now a murder inquiry, and you are the suspects.'

Beside me, Daisy made an appreciative noise. I could tell that she was enjoying the Inspector's sense of theatre.

'I'm afraid, Inspector, that you must be mistaken,' said Miss Griffin calmly.

'I'm afraid that I am not,' said the Inspector, who was just as calm.

Miss Parker's voice, when she spoke, came choking out of her in odd little bursts. 'No,' she said. 'No, she can't be – we argued, I was going to tell her I was sorry – she can't be dead before I've told her how sorry I am!'

Oh, poor Miss Parker, I thought. Daisy sniffed. She did not sound sympathetic.

The Inspector was carrying on. 'The murderer must have been someone who knew her writing well enough to forge a resignation letter, and who had access to Miss

Griffin's desk – in short, it must have been one of the six of you.'

'But this is preposterous!' exclaimed Miss Lappet. She was slurring her words again. 'You have not the smallest bit of evidence against any of us.'

'On the contrary,' said the Inspector. 'I have plenty. There is a bloodstain on the Gym floor and another one on the Gym cupboard's trolley. The disused tunnel under the school bears signs of recent use, including footprints matching Miss Tennyson's shoes, and there is a bloodstain and moss from Oakeshott Woods on Miss Tennyson's abandoned car. I can say with confidence that Miss Tennyson played a part in Miss Bell's death and the disposal of her body. But she did not do it alone.'

I could feel the atmosphere change in the music room, and despite myself I shivered.

'Miss Tennyson's death at first appeared to be a suicide, but certain details did not make sense. There were signs of a struggle, and the body had been rearranged after death. Therefore I deduce that Miss Tennyson's accomplice returned and killed her. Someone in this room is the murderer of *two* women.'

10

'But why do you think one of us did it?' asked Miss Lappet, in a brief moment of clarity. 'It might be anyone.'

'Yes, exactly,' said Miss Hopkins, scandalized. 'Besides, people like us simply don't do that sort of thing.'

'All of you were at school during Monday evening,' the Inspector explained. 'And all of you had a reason to wish Miss Bell dead.'

'Nonsense!' cried Mamzelle suddenly. 'Not *I*, surely! I had no hatred for Mees Bell.'

'Ah, well, that may be true. But you *do* have a secret, don't you?' said the Inspector.

'Whatever do you mean?' asked Mamzelle. Her chin had gone up, and her face was pale. Behind the curtain, Daisy pinched me in excitement. Whatever did the Inspector mean? Had we missed something else?

'This afternoon I wired the school in France you

give as your reference, and they wired back to say that they had never heard of you. In fact, the French do not seem to have any official records of you at all. You aren't Estelle Renauld, are you?'

Behind the curtain I gasped, and Daisy kicked me on the ankle so hard that when I inspected it afterwards I could still see the print of her shoe. All the other staff stared up at Mamzelle in shock. She looked round at them and suddenly burst out laughing.

'The things one will do to get a job,' she said, in a very different accent to her ordinary French one. 'It seemed such a little deception when compared to the reward.'

'You *aren't French?*' shrieked Miss Hopkins.

'I'm from Leicester,' said Mamzelle. 'Down on the official records as Stella Higgins, if you must know. I trained as a Science mistress, but there were no jobs going for a grammar-school girl from Leicester. Then I read about this position. I speak French, after all. My mother was from Toulouse. I thought, why not have a go? It was the sort of place I'd dreamed about teaching at all my life, but I knew I'd never get there as Stella Higgins. So I made a little alteration to my records – taking my mother's maiden name, and changing the spelling of my first name. One of my mother's cousins rewrote my reference so that it came from a school in Provence, and I became Mademoiselle Renauld. But if you think that Miss Bell found out, and I killed her to shut her up, you're quite wrong. I had nothing to do with her death, or Miss Tennyson's – I might have changed my name to get a job, but I'd never *kill* anyone to keep it. And if I'm dismissed for this – well, you're fools. You must admit, I've been good at my job.'

That must have been what Mamzelle was doing when Sophie heard her in the music practice room, I thought. Practising her accent! It had only been a very small mystery, but it was lovely to have it solved.

'Good heavens,' said Miss Hopkins faintly.

'Well,' snapped Miss Griffin. 'We'll deal with this later.'

Inspector Priestley nodded. 'Thank you for clearing that up,' he said to Mamzelle. 'For the moment I shall assume that you are innocent – or rather, that you are guilty of nothing more serious than identity fraud – and move on with the problem of who killed Miss Bell and Miss Tennyson.'

Everyone went very quiet again.

'I didn't do it,' said Miss Parker at last. 'I swear I didn't. Joan and I argued horribly that evening but that's all. I didn't want to tell anyone that we'd had another row – I was embarrassed, so I've been lying about exactly when I left school that day. I was here until nearly six, but I swear I had nothing to do with her being *murdered*. And I thought Joan was alive until just now – didn't I?' she asked The One pleadingly, turning to look at him with huge staring eyes.

The One gulped. 'Miss Parker is telling the truth,' he said. 'Ever since last Tuesday morning she has been asking me to tell her where Miss Bell is. I found it impossible to make her believe that I had no idea, or that I had nothing to do with her resignation.'

I felt pleased again at that. I had guessed right!

'I see,' said the Inspector. 'But why should Miss Parker think that you had something to do with Miss Bell's disappearance?'

'Because Miss Bell told me that she was going to go back to him,' growled Miss Parker, glaring furiously at The One.

'Isn't this exciting?' Daisy whispered to me. 'Just like the end of one of my novels!'

I thought it was more like being at the pictures. After all, there we were in the dark, watching grown-ups weep and shout and accuse each other of dreadful things.

The One went very red. His Adam's apple gulped up and down in his throat, and at first I thought he wasn't going to say anything at all. But then he seemed to decide something. He swallowed once more, and then reached out and put his hand over Miss Hopkins's.

'Miss Bell,' he said unsteadily, 'did come to see me on Monday evening. But, er, I could not possibly give her what she was asking for. You see – when she came in, I was with Arabella. She, er, surprised us together.'

'And what were you doing with Miss Hopkins?' asked the Inspector, although of course he knew perfectly well.

'Er,' said The One sheepishly, 'I'd rather not say, exactly. You see, we are engaged.'

Miss Griffin gave a hiss of rage. 'After all I've done for you!' she said to Miss Hopkins. 'To waste it by getting *married*!'

All I could think was, *They deserve each other.*

'We're going to be married in the spring,' said Miss Hopkins. 'Isn't it blissful? He asked me at lunch last Friday and I said yes. We knew' – she nodded at Miss Griffin – 'that we had to keep it a *deadly* secret. I couldn't wear the ring he bought me, so he gave me these earrings as well, as a token of his love. They are just like the ones Miss Griffin has, which I'd admired. I was so excited about it on Monday that I slipped away from the after-school hockey tactics talk halfway through and went down to his cubby to see him.'

'And what time was that?' asked Inspector Priestley.

'Oh, about five thirty, I should think,' said Miss Hopkins. 'We were there together until just before six.'

The One nodded. 'At one point there was a noise in the corridor and I put my head round the door to see who it was. Miss Tennyson was there, and Mam— er,

Miss . . . er . . . Oh, you remember seeing me, surely?' he asked Mamzelle. She nodded.

'You see?' said Miss Hopkins. 'So we both have alibis. And anyway, there was no reason for either of us to want silly old Miss Bell dead, was there? Not once we were engaged. She might have got cross about it, but she couldn't do anything to us. It would have been perfectly foolish to kill her.'

'Murder is always foolish,' said the Inspector. 'If people only murdered each other rationally, I would be out of a job. Now, what about Miss Lappet and Miss Griffin?'

Miss Lappet twitched back in her seat. 'Miss Griffin and I,' she said faintly, 'were in her office, working on administrative matters. All evening.'

I saw Miss Griffin look at her sideways. *What will she say?* I wondered.

'Yes,' she said after the slightest of pauses. 'Miss Lappet is quite right.'

'How convenient,' said the Inspector politely – not, of course, meaning to be polite at all. 'Thank you. Well, taking all of those statements into account, shall I put forward what I believe happened on Monday evening?'

The room went very still. Daisy bounced silently next to me – I could tell she was holding her hand over her mouth to stop herself from squeaking.

'As I said before, I believe that whoever was responsible for Miss Bell's death was also responsible for Miss Tennyson's – to solve one murder is to solve the other. The crucial person in all this, therefore, is Miss Bell herself. Why would someone have wanted to kill her in the first place?

'Rivalry for the Deputy Headmistress job seems the obvious motive – that would be you, Miss Lappet, as well as Miss Tennyson. Then there is the rather knotty love-life of Mr Reid' – I very nearly giggled at that – 'which involves Mr Reid himself, as well as Miss Parker and Miss Hopkins.'

'I see that I am not included in this little list,' said Miss Griffin frostily. 'Since I am obviously not a suspect, may I be permitted to leave?'

'Certainly not,' snapped the Inspector. 'Two of your mistresses have died in the past week. If nothing else, as Headmistress you should take responsibility for their welfare.'

'Come now, Inspector,' said Miss Griffin. 'It is rather hard to run a school with no mistresses. I hardly think it would be in my best interests to kill my own staff.'

'Indeed,' said the Inspector. 'For a headmistress to kill her own staff she would have to have a very good reason.'

'Exactly,' said Miss Griffin, sitting back in her chair.

'Exactly,' the Inspector echoed. 'So. *Did* you have a very good reason for doing it?'

Suddenly the rest of the mistresses began to catch on to what was happening. They all whipped their heads round to stare at Miss Griffin, like people at a tennis match.

'Certainly not!' It was almost a shout.

'It seems to me,' the Inspector went on smoothly, 'that Miss Bell must have been a rather desperate woman. She needed money, did she not? That's why she was performing secretarial duties for you. After she was rejected by Mr Reid, that Deputy job must have become even more important to her. If she had known anything that could have swung the appointment in her favour, or given her more power at Deepdean, I suspect she would have used it. So, *did* she know something about your past that you might want to keep hidden?'

'Do – not – be – ridiculous,' hissed Miss Griffin. 'As I have told you, I was in my office all Monday evening with Miss Lappet.'

'I think you'll find that it was Miss Lappet who told me you were meeting in your office all evening – a tale, incidentally, that I find suspiciously convenient and not particularly likely. I suggest that after a very brief meeting in your office, Miss Lappet left – witnessed by several of your students, I might add – and then spent much of the evening in another room, perhaps with a bottle to keep her company. Leaving *you* on your own.'

Oh! I thought. Of course, that made sense. If Miss Lappet had been off somewhere drinking, she would not want anyone to know about it. That was why she had made up the story about being with Miss Griffin all evening. And of course, it had suited Miss Griffin to play along with that.

'It isn't true!' shouted Miss Lappet. 'It isn't – what I mean to say is, I was only out of the room for a little while. A very little while. And I only had a nip of something, the merest nip – I resent your implications. Resent them!'

'Oh, do be quiet, Elizabeth,' hissed Miss Griffin.

Miss Lappet flinched and pushed her glasses up her nose. The Inspector looked rather pleased with himself.

'Indeed,' he said. 'And with that, Miss Griffin, your alibi vanishes. Now, I believe that you met Miss Bell on the Gym balcony. During that meeting, she threatened you with blackmail. You argued with her, and then you reached out and pushed her over the side.'

11

Inspector Priestley stopped for a moment. The whole room was horribly, heavily silent, as though electricity was crackling round the edges and sparking from person to person. I could hear myself breathing and my heart pounding – I was terrified all over again.

Miss Griffin sat glaring straight ahead, her jaw clenched shut and her fingers white on her lap, but everyone else stared towards her, like people at a tennis match after the last point has been played.

'Nonsense,' she said, in an icy-cold voice. 'This is all nonsense. You have no proof.'

'Miss Bell asked to see you that evening,' said Mamzelle suddenly. 'I remember now. It was in the mistresses' common room – I was there.'

'Be *quiet*,' snarled Miss Griffin.

'I certainly shall not,' said Mamzelle, offended. 'What I said is true and I'm prepared to say so in court.'

'And you think they'll believe you? You're not even French!'

'I told you I liked Mamzelle,' I whispered in Daisy's ear.

'Shh – he hasn't got her in the bag yet,' Daisy whispered back.

'Quite apart from witness statements,' the Inspector was saying, unruffled, 'I can have Miss Bell's resignation letter and Miss Tennyson's suicide note tested against your handwriting. My men are fingerprinting Miss Tennyson's car and the Gym cupboard trolley to match to your prints.'

'I've destroyed the resignation letter,' snapped Miss Griffin. 'And those prints could have got there at any time.'

'The woman who runs Miss Tennyson's boarding house has also identified you from a photograph as the woman who came to visit her on Saturday evening,' the Inspector went on.

'No one can tell anything from a photograph – that's common knowledge!'

Despite myself, I was rather impressed by the way Miss Griffin was brazening it out. I certainly wouldn't have been able to lie so quickly and well. She must, I thought, have had a lot of practice.

'And your fingerprints have also been found on Miss Tennyson's bottle of Veronal.'

Miss Griffin made a most unladylike snort. 'This is ridiculous. Are you expecting me to slip up and tell you that I was wearing gloves? Now, you can accuse me of what you like, but I don't believe you could even bring this to trial. If you were hoping for a confession, I'm afraid you will be disappointed.'

And she smiled. It was the most terrifying smile I have ever seen. It looked like it came from a person made out of clockwork.

'Ah,' said Inspector Priestley. 'But I do have one more piece of evidence that may sway you.' And he took out Verity's diary.

Miss Hopkins whispered, 'Oh, what *is* it?' to The One, as though she were watching a play.

Miss Griffin did not do anything all, but her face went tight all over.

'This diary,' said the Inspector, 'is what Miss Bell intended to use for blackmail. It makes for astonishing reading – as I assume, Miss Griffin, you know. I assume you also know that, on its own, this is enough to have you removed from the school, to ensure that you never teach again, and even possibly to convict you of a previous crime. Its contents also provide the perfect motive for the two murders you have carried out. And that is my case against you.'

12

When we talked about it afterwards, Daisy swore that at the end of his speech, Inspector Priestley bowed, like a magician who has just finished a trick – but I think that is only what she herself would have done. At any rate, no one was looking at the Inspector then. They were staring at Miss Griffin. She had begun to shake, like a clockwork person coming unwound, and was making odd little hissing noises out of the side of her mouth.

'How did you find it?' she asked jerkily. 'How did you know – who told you – *I have been looking for that diary everywhere!*'

'I'm afraid I'm not in the habit of revealing my sources,' said the Inspector.

Miss Griffin stared around, as though she was looking for the first time – at Miss Lappet, who was shivering in her seat, like a jelly wobbling, at Miss Hopkins, clutching The One's arm for protection, at Miss Parker, who was slowly turning purple with rage, at Mamzelle, who looked as though she had found something nasty on her shoe; and then she turned her head to stare at the velvet curtain we were hiding behind. I swear she looked straight at me.

I jerked back into the stuffy dark, making the edge of the curtain move, and she must have seen it, even if she had not been sure before.

'Chump!' gasped Daisy. She did not stop watching, of course. It would have taken more than that to make Daisy stop looking at something so interesting.

From the room beyond I heard a voice that sounded barely human, shouting something. It took me a moment to make out the words, '*WELLS! WONG!*'

Something banged on the floor, there was a scuffle, the sound of voices and a *thump*, and then I heard the Inspector, very close to our curtain, saying, 'I am arresting you for attempting to assault an officer of the law, and also for involvement in the deaths of Joan Bell, Amelia Tennyson and Verity Abraham. Come quietly and I shan't have to do anything I might regret later.'

There was a pause, and then, 'He's got her,' breathed Daisy ecstatically. '*Spiffing.*'

And that was the end of Miss Griffin.

It's odd to think that this is so nearly over. I found Miss Bell in the Gym on the 29th of October, and now it is the 18th of December and Christmas is next week. I am at Fallingford, Daisy's home. Paper chains are being put up everywhere, great big spicy branches are being hauled in from outside and wrapped round the banisters, and there are great trays of biscuits and cakes coming out of the kitchen. The dogs keep trying to eat them, which makes Daisy's mother quite cross.

Last term was really finished on the day that I have just described. For a while we all thought that Deepdean might be over too. After what we saw in the music room, Daisy and I were given a police escort back up to House. The tall, stern policeman took us, as Inspector Priestley was busy arresting Miss Griffin. The tall policeman told us not to breathe a word to anyone on pain of death (I think he was joking, but I am not sure), but by the time school ended on Tuesday afternoon, everyone already knew that Miss Griffin had been arrested for murdering Miss Bell and Miss Tennyson.

Some second formers had seen the handcuffed Miss Griffin being led away to a police car, so – as much as the masters and mistresses tried to hide it – the cat was well and truly out of the bag. Quite a few people refused to believe she had committed the murders at first, and there were lots of conspiracy theories about sinister gangs, but in the end, as more bits and pieces came out, everyone began to accept that it must be true.

From that day onwards all the grown-ups seemed to

forget about us – even Matron was busy giving her statement to the police – so meals came at odd times and we were left to hang about doing nothing. We played rounds and rounds of cards in the House common room and gossiped about the murders. I knew that Daisy was dying to brag about our part in the case, but because we had promised the Inspector, she bit her tongue, and we both did very good impressions of people who knew no more about it than the next girl.

In a way, I can still hardly believe it. That episode in the music room really has become a sort of film scene in my head. Perhaps it stops me from feeling so frightened about the events that led up to it. Daisy, of course, thinks that's silly.

Miss Hopkins is leaving Deepdean. She is going away to Derbyshire to live with The One after they are married. Miss Parker is going away too, to teach in London. I think it is too painful for her to be here any more.

When we first heard all this, at the end of November, we really did think that Deepdean might be over for ever. 'After all,' said Kitty, 'we've no mistresses left, so if we do come back next term we shall be teaching ourselves.' Mothers came down in droves that week to take girls away. Beanie went, and Kitty, and half of the rest of our form.

Then Miss Lappet made her announcement. She

called all those girls still at school down to the Hall and told us that Mamzelle was going to be the new Deputy Headmistress. Miss Lappet herself will help Mamzelle hunt for a new headmistress, and new mistresses, during this holiday, and in January the school will reopen for everyone who wants to come back. Mamzelle, by the way, is still Mamzelle, French accent and all. Miss Lappet seems smaller and sadder, but she no longer has her strong after-dinner smell, and when she looks at you both her eyes focus on your face.

After all that news, term was officially over. Letters were sent out to parents explaining things as nicely as possible and asking them to take the rest of us away. I didn't know what I was going to do. At the beginning of the year my father had arranged for me to stay at House over the holidays, but under the circumstances that now seemed rather unlikely.

I was still worrying about it when Daisy got a telegram that said:

DARLING SO GLAD YOU ARE NOT
DEAD COMMA MUST YOU REALLY
COME HOME NOW THOUGH HAD
PLANNED GOING LONDON MOST
INCONVENIENT STOP KISSES
MUMMY

Daisy read it and sighed. 'Mummy thinks telegrams are very now,' she said, 'only I can't make her understand how they ought to read. I suppose I shall have to telephone her – she'll be very awkward about it if we simply turn up.'

'We?' I asked.

'Of course, *we*. You don't think I'd let you rot in House, with just ugly old Matron for company over Christmas, do you?'

Matron gave Daisy the telephone, grumbling rather but wanting very much to be rid of us, and I stood by while Daisy asked the operator for Fallingford 123. The phone rang, and was picked up, and Daisy said: 'Hello, Chapman, is Mummy there? It's – yes – could you . . . ? Mummy? Mummy, it's Daisy. Yes – I know – Mummy, you simply must send O'Brian to collect us, they won't have us here any more . . . Mummy, the school is *closing* . . . Yes, I know I'm perfectly all right, but Mummy, listen . . . Oh, *us*? My friend Hazel, she's coming to stay over Christmas. She can sleep in the nursery with me . . . Oh, Mummy, honestly, you can still go to London if we're there, just send along O'Brian now and you can have him tomorrow . . . Yes . . . yes . . . oh, good. Goodbye, Mummy.'

'Mummy,' said Daisy after she had put the phone down, 'is sometimes quite difficult to manage. O'Brian will be here in an hour.'

After that, we had a frantic rush gathering all our things together. It didn't work out perfectly – I came away with Kitty's school hat and Lavinia's history book – but when O'Brian pulled up in the drive an hour later we were sitting on our trunks waiting for him. We drove away down Oakeshott Hill, past the closed-up doors of Deepdean – and that, really, is the end of this story.

There are just a few more things to say.

The first is that, last week, we had a visit from King Henry. As I said, she lives not far from Daisy, so Daisy's parents were not at all surprised when she came for tea. I'm not sure how they would have reacted if they could have heard what King Henry told us once Hetty the maid had brought in the tea things and left the room.

'I wanted to say – well, that I think you're both bricks. Utter bricks. I can't thank you enough.'

'Did you *know*?' asked Daisy, spinning her teacup in its saucer excitedly.

King Henry shook her lovely curls. 'No,' she said. 'I never knew, exactly. I only guessed – and how I hoped I was wrong! When Verity died, it was so awful—' She broke off and had to take a sip of tea to calm down. 'I didn't know what to believe. I knew that she couldn't have done it to herself, but if she hadn't . . . I hoped it was an accident. I mean, *Miss Griffin*!'

'Oh, I know,' said Daisy feelingly.

'I felt terribly bad, taking the Head Girl post when she offered it to me, but because I wasn't *sure*, of course there was nothing I could say. Then Miss Bell disappeared, and I had the most dreadful feeling, as though it was Verity, all over again. I knew that Miss Griffin had something to do with it, but of course I had no proof. Then Miss Tennyson asked me to meet her in the Willow, and said that she had something to tell me. I was terrified, but I went – and then I saw you, and I simply lost my nerve. When I heard on Monday that *she* was dead too, I nearly fainted. I was sure I'd be next. Honestly, when I heard from that nice Inspector about what you did, what you proved – I realized that you simply saved my life.'

'Oh no, it was nothing,' said Daisy, preening.

'It certainly *was* something. On behalf of the whole of Deepdean,' said King Henry, ignoring her, 'I salute you.'

So, in a way, I suppose that Daisy and I *did* get our praise.

The Inspector came to visit us at Fallingford a few days later, to tell us more about the case. He even let us read a copy of Miss Griffin's confession. It was very odd, seeing Miss Griffin's words down on the page like that. Miss Tennyson had been dragged into it because she had caught sight of Miss Griffin in Library corridor that evening, all bloody, and Miss Griffin had offered Miss Tennyson the Deputy job in return for not ratting her out. The confession also said that it was a mistake, her pushing Verity, which made me feel sorry for her. Daisy told me to stop being soft about it, especially since Miss Bell and Miss Tennyson's murders had not been mistakes at all.

Miss Griffin is in prison in London, and her sentencing will be some time early next year. I don't think I want to go, although Daisy does, of course. I don't like to think of what is waiting for Miss Griffin at the end of it all.

Daisy says that it should not upset me. It is no more than Miss Griffin deserves. I don't know if I agree with her.

After the Inspector left, Daisy's mother came in. She was dressed for dinner in an arsenic-green silk gown and a real mink wrap. She looked very glamorous, and just like Daisy, only much older and much more vague.

'*What* a handsome man,' she said. 'Why ever did he come?'

'I have told you, Mummy,' said Daisy reproachfully. 'He was that policeman from the case. He came by to make sure we were all right. They're visiting all the girls.'

I still can never believe how Daisy can lie to her parents like that, bare-faced and not even blinking.

'How kind of him,' said her mother, yawning and adjusting her pearls. 'I'm glad it was only that, you know. I wouldn't like to think of you mixed up in one of those nasty police investigations. He really was quite criminally handsome, though. Do you think he'll come back again anytime soon?'

'I do hope so, Mummy,' said Daisy, at her most virtuous. 'He really is a very interesting sort of person.'

And her mother wandered out of the room and left us alone, in fits of giggles.

Daisy's Guide to Deepdean

Hello. Hazel has asked me to write a dictionary explaining particular words in her case notes. Honestly, I don't think much of the words she has chosen, but I have done it – and I've added in some useful information for any girl who wants to get on at Deepdean.

- **Bunbreak** – this happens every school morning at 11. We are given biscuits or buns and allowed to run about outside for ten minutes exactly. The best bunbreak food is quite clearly squashed fly biscuits. Hazel doesn't like them, which is proof of how often Hazel is wrong. It is important not to be at the back of the bunbreak queue, otherwise someone else might take your biscuits.

- **Bull's eyes** – these are sweets. They are striped and minty, and they crunch when you bite them.

- **Canoodling** – a grown-up sort of kissing behind closed doors.

317

- **Card** – a girl who is amusing. You should be a card exactly the right amount of time, but not more. I am a card three times a day, and twice on Sundays.

- **Chump** – an idiot. Sometimes Hazel can be this. You should try to avoid it.

- **Common Room** – a room where people go to enjoy themselves. The mistresses have one, and we have our own up at House. (Of course, the mistresses' is better.)

- **Confiscation** – this is a nice word for having something taken away from you by the mistresses or by Matron because you are not supposed to own it. It is very annoying. If you have something illegal, you should always keep it in a very clever hiding place.

- **Div.** – this is short for Divinity, and it means the religious lessons we go to with Mr Maclean. I already know the Bible, though, so I don't see what the point is.

- **Dorm** – a room in House where girls sleep. When you are shrimps you sleep all together in a very large dorm, but as you become a bigger girl you are allowed to pick your dorm mates.

- **Dunce** – a girl who is no good at lessons, no matter how hard she tries.

- **Hols** – when you are not at school, you are on hols. I am always given a governess during the holidays, who makes sure that I don't disturb Mummy. Mummy, needless to say, is always on hols.

- **House** – where you change your clothes and sleep and eat your dinner while you are at school. It is not your real house – they only call it this to trick the shrimps into thinking that it is a nice, safe home. This is a scam.

- **Jilting** – throwing someone over, instead of marrying them.

- **Keeping mum** – not telling what you shouldn't. If you do tell, you are a rat, and everyone is allowed to hate you.

- **Lacrosse** – quite simply the best sport ever invented. You play it with sticks that have a net at one end, which you use to catch the ball and lob it into the other team's goal. Heaven.

- **Master** – a Deepdean word for men who are teachers.

- **Matron** – matrons come with school Houses. All they care about is telling you to brush your hair and clean your face. Our matron is always confiscating our tuck and then eating it herself, because she is a greedy pig.

- **Mistress** – a Deepdean word for lady teachers.

- **Mufti** – your home clothes, for when you're not wearing your uniform.

- **Pavilion** – the small building where we change our clothes before and after Games, and where tactics sessions are held before matches.

- **Pinafore** – the dull grey dress that we wear as part of our uniform.

- **Prayers** – every day before lessons we have to go to the school Hall and sit through Prayers. We sing a hymn, listen to a speech, and it is important to look as though you are paying attention.

- **Prep** – extra work that the mistresses give us to do between lessons. It is best to pretend you have not finished this, even when you have, otherwise you will be thought a swot.

- **Pullover** – a jumper that we wear as part of our uniform.

- **San** – where you go when you are pretending to be ill, or when you fall over and cut yourself. It is looked after by a nurse. Our nurse, Minny, is a pet.

- **Shrimps** – these are the smallest girls. I suppose I was a shrimp once, but it is hard to believe that I was ever as stupid as the shrimps are today.

- **Socs** – after-school societies. There are societies for History, Drama, and English, and it is very important to join one if you want to get on.

- **Squashed fly** – these are the very best kind of biscuit you can be given at bunbreak. The flies are not flies at all, but raisins.

- **Swot** – a girl who tries too hard at lessons. It is very important not to be one if you want to be someone at Deepdean.

- **Tongue** – I don't know why Hazel has put this word in! It is exactly what it says. It is a cow's tongue, and it is for eating. Honestly, Hazel. Fancy not knowing something like that!

- **Tuck** – sweets and cakes, kept in a tuck box under your bed. You can keep anything in your tuck box, but make sure never to keep illegal things in there because Matron will find them straight away. It is a very stupid hiding place.

- **View–halloo!** – this is a hunting word, and it means that you have found a fox and are chasing it. It can also be shouted when you are being a detective, to show that you have reached the good bit in the story and are about to catch the murderer.

ACKNOWLEDGMENTS

Every book I write is really for my parents. For my father, for teaching me to love language and putting every book that matters to me into my hands when I was a child, and for my mother, for faithfully reading every word that I wrote as a result (even the bad ones). *Murder Most Unladylike* would not exist without them.

I began to write this book in 2011, for NaNoWriMo. Most of the first draft happened in the break room of the Oxford branch of Blackwell's Bookstore – so thank you, so much, to each one of my amazing and talented colleagues there, and especially to Rebecca Waiting, children's bookseller extraordinaire.

Thank you also to my early readers, most especially Rebecca Stevens, Boadicea Meath Baker (who also supplied me with extensive period detail and a historically accurate writing soundtrack), Fleur Frederick, and Moniza Hossein (who courageously read all 85,000 words of the first draft while sick with flu). I salute them all, and I hope it's better now.

Many thanks to my large and lovely family, every last one of you, and to my friends, who bear with me wonderfully and who all played a part in *Murder Most Unladylike* (even though they probably don't know it). Alice, Alison, Amy, Ana, Damien, Emily, Emma (all of you), Jeff, Julia, Laurence, Max, Owain, Priya, Richard, Sarah (ALL of you), Scarlett, Zara and everyone else. Thank you especially to Matthew, for being surprisingly willing to live with me and love me even though my head is full of books, and to the whole Smalley family, for making me feel so welcome.

I have been very lucky in my publishers. Thank you to the fantastic Natalie Doherty, Annie Eaton and the whole team at Random House, who have made my publishing process feel like a dream. My books could not have found a better or more enthusiastic home. Thanks also to the delightful Kristin Ostby and the team at S&S US, for welcoming Hazel and Daisy to America in such style. And of course, to my other publishing family at Orion, especially Amber Caravéo and Fiona Kennedy, huge thanks – they have taught me so well, and they have been so willing to harbour an author in their editorial ranks.

This book, and I, though, would still be lost if it were not for one marvellous woman: my agent, Gemma Cooper. She fell for Hazel and Daisy and she changed my life. There aren't words to express my gratitude. There never will be. Thank you.

Robin Stevens, Cambridge and London, 2013

Turn over to read an extract from Daisy and
Hazel's next thrilling mystery:

1

Something dreadful has happened to Mr Curtis.

I am quite surprised to realize that I mind. If you had asked me this morning what I thought of him, I should have told you that Mr Curtis was not a nice man at all. But not even the nastiest person deserves this.

Of course, Daisy doesn't see it like that. To her, crimes are not real things to be upset about. She is only interested in the fact that something has *happened*, and she wants to understand what it means. So do I, of course – I wouldn't be a proper member of the Detective Society if I didn't – but no matter how hard I try, I can't *only* think like a detective.

The fact is, Daisy and I will both need to think like detectives again. You see, just now we overheard something quite awful; something that proves that what happened to Mr Curtis was not simply an accident, or a sudden illness. Someone did this to him, and that can only mean one thing: the Detective Society has a brand-new case to investigate.

Daisy has ordered me to write what we have found out so far in the Detective Society's casebook. She is always on about the importance of taking notes – and also very sure that *she* should not have to take them. Notes are up to me – I am the Society's Secretary, as well as its Vice-President, and Daisy is its President. Although I am just as good a detective as she is – I proved that during our first real case, the Murder of Miss Bell – I am a quite different sort of person to Daisy. I like thinking about things before I act, while Daisy always has to go rushing head over heels into things like a dog after a rabbit, and that doesn't leave much time for note-making. We are entirely different to look at, too: I am dark-haired and short and round, and Daisy is whippet-thin and tall, with glorious golden hair. But all the same, we are best friends, and an excellent crime-detecting partnership.

I think I had better hurry up and explain what has happened, and who Mr Curtis is.

I suppose it all began when I came to Daisy's house, Fallingford, for the Easter holidays and her birthday.

2

Spring term at our school, Deepdean, had been quite safe and ordinary. That was surprising after everything that had happened there last year – I mean the murder, and then the awful business with the school nearly closing down. But the spring term was quite peaceful, without any hint of danger or death, and I was very glad. The most exciting case we had investigated recently was the Case of the Frog in Kitty's Bed.

I was expecting Fallingford to be just as calm. Fallingford, for this new casebook, is Daisy's house: a proper English country mansion, with wood-panelled walls and acres of sprawling grounds with a maze and even an enormous monkey puzzle tree in the middle of the front drive. At first I thought the tree was a fake, but then I investigated and it is quite real.

Honestly, Fallingford is just like a house in a book. It has its own woods and lake, four sets of stairs (Daisy thinks there must be a secret passageway too, only she has never discovered it) and a walled kitchen garden just as hidden as Mary Lennox's in the book. From the outside it is a great grand square of warm yellow stone that people have been busily adding to for hundreds of years; the inside is a magic box of rooms and staircases and corridors, all unfolding and leading into each other three ways at once. There are whole flocks of stuffed birds (most especially a stuffed owl on the first-floor landing), a grand piano, several Spanish chests and even a real suit of armour in the hall. Just like at Deepdean, everything is treated so carelessly, and is so old and battered, that it took me a while to realize how valuable all these things really are. Daisy's mother leaves her jewels about on her dressing table, the dogs are dried off after muddy walks with towels that were a wedding present to Daisy's grandmother from the King, and Daisy dog-ears the first-edition books in the library. Nothing is younger than Daisy's father, and it makes my family's glossy white wedding-cake compound in Hong Kong look as if it is only pretending to be real.

We arrived in the family car, driven by the chauffeur, O'Brian (who is also the gardener – unlike our family, the Wellses don't seem to have quite enough servants, and I wonder whether this also has something to do with the fading state of the house), on a sunny Saturday morning, the sixth of April. We came out of the light into the big dark hallway (stone-floored, with the suit of armour looming out at you alarmingly from the dimness), and Chapman, the Wellses' old butler, was there to greet us. He is white-haired and stooping, and he has been in the family so long that he is beginning to run down, just like the grandfather clock. The two dogs were there too – the little spaniel, Millie, bouncing around Daisy's knees, and the fat old yellow Labrador, Toast Dog, rocking back and forth on his stiff legs and making groaning noises as though he were ill. Chapman bent down to pick up Daisy's tuck box with a groan just like Toast Dog's (he really is very old – I kept worrying that he would seize up in the middle of something like a rusty toy) and said, 'Miss Daisy, it's good to have you home.'

Then Daisy's father came bounding out of the library. Lord Hastings (*Lord Hastings* is what Daisy's father is called, although his last name is Wells, like Daisy – apparently, when you are made a lord, you are given an extra name to show how important you are) has fat pink cheeks, a fat white moustache and a stomach that strains against his tweed jackets, but when he smiles, he looks just like Daisy.

'Daughter!' he shouted, holding out his arms. 'Daughter's friend! Do I know you?'

Daisy's father is very forgetful.

'Of course you know Hazel, Daddy,' said Daisy, sighing. 'She came for Christmas.'

7

'Hazel! Welcome, welcome. How are you? *Who* are you? You don't look like Daisy's friends usually do. Are you English?'

'She's from Hong Kong, Daddy,' said Daisy. 'She can't help it.'

I squeezed my fingers tight around the handles of my travelling case and tried to keep smiling. I am so used to being at Deepdean now – and everyone there is so used to me – that I can sometimes forget that I'm different. But as soon as I leave school I remember all over again. The first time people see me they stare at me and sometimes say things under their breath. Usually they say them out loud. I know it is the way things are, but I wish I was not the only one of me – and I wish that the *me* I am did not seem like the wrong sort of *me* to be.

'My name is Lord Hastings,' said Lord Hastings, obviously trying to be helpful, 'but you may call me Daisy's father, because that is who I am.'

'She knows, Daddy!' said Daisy. 'I told you, she's been here before.'

'Well, I'm terribly pleased you're both here now,' said her father. 'Come through to the library.' He was bouncing up and down on his toes, his cheeks all scrunched up above his moustache.

Daisy looked at him suspiciously. 'If this is one of your tricks . . .' she said.

'Oh, come along, tiresome child.' He put out his arm

8

and Daisy, grinning, took it like a lady being escorted in to dinner.

Lord Hastings led her out of the hall and into the library. I followed on behind. It's warmer in there, and the shelves are lined with battered and well-read leather books. It is odd to compare it to my father's library, where everything matches, and is dusted twice daily by one of the valets. Fallingford really is as untidy as the inside of Daisy's head.

Lord Hastings motioned Daisy into a fat green chair, scattered with cushions. She sat gracefully – and there was a loud and very rude sound.

Lord Hastings roared with laughter. 'Isn't it good?' he cried. 'I saw it in the *Boy's Own Paper* and sent off for it at once.'

Daisy groaned. 'Daddy,' she said, 'you are an awful fool.'

'Oh, come now, Daisy dearest. It's an excellent joke. Sometimes I wonder whether you are a child at all.'

Daisy drew herself up to her full height. 'Really, Daddy,' she said, 'I shouldn't think there's room for *another* child in this house.' But she was grinning again, and Lord Hastings twinkled back.

'Now, come along, Hazel, I think we ought to go up to our room.'

And off we went.

3

Lord Hastings kept on playing humorous jokes all week. 'Daddy,' groaned Daisy as she picked a splash of fake ink off her dinner plate on Tuesday, 'you are an embarrassment to me.' But I could tell, from the way she looked at him as he giggled into his handkerchief, that she didn't mean it. Although the careful, good-show Daisy was still in place whenever her mother was watching, I noticed that her secret side, clever and fiercely interested in everything, kept popping out around Lord Hastings – and that, I knew, meant something. Daisy only shows her real self to people she truly likes, and there are not many of them at all. At dinner that day, though, Lady Hastings was there – and so Daisy was careful to be absolutely proper.

'*Really*, George,' snapped Lady Hastings, glaring at her husband.

We all cringed a bit. There was something very

wrong between Lord and Lady Hastings this hols. At Christmas I had thought Daisy's mother perfectly nice, if slightly vague, but this time she was quite different – all brittle and angry at everything. She was still just as tall and blonde and glamorously beautiful as she had been at Christmas, but now her beauty was like a porcelain vase that must not be touched. Everything Lord Hastings did seemed to be wrong. Staying in the house with them was a bit like being stuck in the middle of a war, with troops on either side sending shells over our heads. I know all about parents not speaking – at home there are weeks when my mother and father talk to each other through me, as though I'm a living telephone – but this seemed to be something else entirely. Poor Lord Hastings drooped. Hopeful presents of sagging flowers and squashed chocolates kept appearing outside Lady Hastings' room, and then were banished straight down to the kitchens, which began to look very much like the inside of a hot-house. Daisy and I ate most of the chocolates for our bunbreaks (Daisy insisted on having bunbreaks in the hols, 'in honour of Deepdean', and I saw no reason to argue with her).

'He loves her,' said Daisy, munching an orange cream, 'and she loves him too, really, only she sometimes doesn't show it. She'll come round in the end.'

I wasn't so sure. Lady Hastings seemed to spend all her time either locked away in her bedroom or on the telephone in the hall, whispering away into it and falling silent when we came too close.

It was not just Daisy and I who had been turned into hostages of the row between her parents. Daisy's brother Bertie, who was in his final year at Eton, was home for the holidays too.

Bertie looked unnervingly like Daisy – a Daisy stretched out like India rubber and shorn of her hair – but if Daisy fizzed like a rocket, Bertie hummed with rage. He was cross all the time, and as soon as he arrived he began to crash about the house. He had a pair of bright green trousers, an out-of-tune ukulele which he insisted on playing at odd hours of the day and night (according to Daisy he could only play three songs, and they were all rude), and a friend whose name was Stephen Bampton.

I felt very grateful that Stephen was *not* a cross person. He was short and stocky, with smooth reddish hair, and he seemed gentle and slightly sad. He looked at me as though I were a *person* rather than The Orient, and I liked him at once.

I was glad he was there, because this hols, Fallingford felt foreign – or perhaps it reminded me how foreign *I* was. Bertie jangled away on his ukulele, musically angry, and Lord and Lady Hastings argued, and Daisy went bouncing around the house, showing me secret hiding places and house-martin nests and a sword that had belonged to her great-grandfather, and I began to be hungry for my own Hong Kong house's gluey heat and fake flower arrangements.

The last person in the house – apart from the cook and housekeeper, Mrs Doherty, and Hetty the maid – was Miss Alston, Daisy's governess. There was always a governess in the holidays at Deepdean, to help Daisy with prep and keep her out of trouble – and to help Lord Hastings write letters. 'He gets muddled when he tries to do it himself, poor dear,' Daisy told me, by way of explanation.

This hols, though, dull, droning Miss Rose, who we'd had to suffer at Christmas, had quite inexplicably gone away. 'With only the briefest telephone call!' said Lady Hastings, as cross as ever. 'Really!' Instead, we had Miss Alston.

Miss Alston was, as our Deepdean dorm mate Kitty would have said, a frump. She was the very image of a spinster bluestocking: she wore ugly square clothes without a waist, her hair stood out from her forehead in a heavy clump, and she always carried an enormous handbag in ugly brown pigskin. On first acquaintance, she seemed very safe and very dull, but that was misleading. The more lessons we had with her, the more we realized that Miss Alston was not dull at all. She was interesting.

Miss Rose had simply marched us through our

Deepdean prep like an army general with no time to waste, but Miss Alston was not like that at all. If we were working on a Latin translation about Hannibal, she would stop to talk about his elephants. If we were learning about water, she took us outside to look at the clouds. If we were reading a Shakespeare play, she asked us whether we felt sorry for the Macbeths. I said yes (though they shouldn't have done it), and Daisy said absolutely not, of course. 'Explain,' said Miss Alston, and for almost half an hour we both quite forgot that we were doing prep, in the holidays, with a governess.

The oddest thing was that, around the grown-ups, Miss Alston was very different. She was perfectly ordinary. When she wasn't busy with us, she sat with Lord Hastings, drafting his letters and making lists and ordering him yo-yos and fake moustaches from his *Boy's Own* catalogues. He thought Miss Alston deadly dull, just as Daisy and I had before she began teaching us. 'She doesn't even laugh at my jokes!' he complained.

'I shouldn't think *that* was a surprise,' said Daisy, patting him on the head as if she were stroking Toast Dog. 'Mummy, where did you find Miss Alston?'

'Goodness, how should I remember?' asked Lady Hastings, who was busy trying to brush dog hair off her cape. 'The agency, I suppose. There was a letter . . . Heavens, Daisy, why must you complain about your governesses? You know perfectly well that I can't look after you.'

'Quite obviously,' said Daisy icily. I knew what lay behind the question. Daisy wanted to understand Miss Alston, and what made her so different – but there was no easy answer to that. Miss Alston kept on being privately interesting and publicly dull, and Daisy and I became more and more curious about her.